VERDIGRIS

Verdigris

MICHELE MARI

*Translated from the Italian
by Brian Robert Moore*

SHEFFIELD – LONDON – NEW YORK

First published in English in 2024 by And Other Stories
Sheffield – London – New York
www.andotherstories.org

.1 3 5 7 9 8 6 4 2

ISBN: 9781913505905
eBook ISBN: 9781913505912

Editor: Jeremy M. Davies; Copy-editor: Gesche Ipsen; Proofreader: Sarah Terry;
Typesetter: Tetragon, London; Typefaces: Albertan Pro and Linotype Syntax
(interior) and Stellage (cover); Series Cover Design: Elisa von Randow,
Alles Blau Studio, Brazil, after a concept by And Other Stories;

And Other Stories books are printed and bound in the UK on FSC-certified
paper by Clays Ltd. The covers are of G . F Smith 270gsm Colorplan
card, which is sustainably manufactured at the James Cropper paper
mill in the Lake District, and are stamped with biodegradable foil.

A catalogue record for this book is available from the British Library.

And Other Stories gratefully acknowledge that our work is supported
using public funding by Arts Council England and that the translation
of this book was partially funded by the support of a grant from English
PEN's PEN Translates programme, which is supported by Arts Council
England. This work has been translated with the contribution of the Italian
Ministry of Culture' Centre for Books and Reading (CEPELL).

Bisected by a precise blow of the spade, the slug writhed a moment longer: then it moved no more. All its glittering viscosity was left in its wake, for the split instead revealed a dry and compact surface, whose purplish-brown hue made it resemble the sliced end of a miniature bresaola. So, the animal needed to rid itself continuously of its slimy shame in order to maintain an inner purity, and fruit of this noble punishment was the metamorphosis of that foul ejection into splendidly iridescent shards.

Corrugated with parallel and regular grooves, its integument had a reddish color reminiscent of a bolete, a characteristic that distinguished the mollusk in question as a red slug, or rather, a French slug: stubbier and lighter than the local variety, with a silhouette closer to a whale's than to a serpent's, and with shorter horns less given to protrusion.

"Blech!" exclaimed the churl, spitting on the tiny cadaver but missing it by a few centimeters. Then he pulled back the spade and slid its blade between two fingers, as if to clean it of a slime that existed only in his mind. "Frensh slug!"—and once again there exploded forth a clot of saliva that, like the preceding gob, no benediction could have transformed into mother-of-pearl. "Cripes, be a nasty slug!" And finally he walked away.

I, too, walked away, only to come back a few hours later to witness the work of the ants, which, having completely covered the two stumps of the slug, sucked out its lifeblood, reducing the remains to a bundle of mummified fibers. I liked to think of those tiny creatures as the crew of the *Pequod* engaged in carving a cetacean, and from this thought took shape the irresistible image of a mammoth white slug riddled with scars, the slug of vengeance . . .

Too bad that my country fellow had nothing of Captain Ahab about him. Rather, he was characterized by a kind of formless-ness, both in his corpulence, perennially enveloped in the same bluish coverall, and in his face, which was complicated by a scar running from the lashes of his left eye to his lip, by a vast birthmark colored the purplish tint of wine sediment, and by his many warts, whose protuberance was counterbalanced by the chasmic concavity of his smallpox ulcers. Markedly wrecked was his nose, knobby and spongelike as though due to a cirrhotic liver, and covered by a network of little dark veins. Unpleasantly teary were his eyes, with lids almost glued together by resin, apparently from chronic pinkeye: a phenomenon that, at the very least, granted him a pensive and concentrated air, like someone gazing with his mind's eye at metaphysical distances.

In my head, I called him the verdigris man, because of all his tasks—which included the tending of the vegetable garden and trees, the minimal upkeep of the house, the cutting of the grass, and the farming of chickens and rabbits—for a young boy, the preparing and the spraying of verdigris was the most enchanting. I would see him break up clumps of solid verdigris in a metal bin, and each one of those fragments held the sinister seduction of the colored chalks that proved fatal for Mimì, the "silly girl" from the nursery rhyme. Awful punishments awaited, were I to lay but a finger on one of those fragments; and yet, seeing as he handled them with his bare hands, drawing from them a turquoise that not only tinted his skin but settled permanently under his fingernails, the possibilities were twofold: either the verdigris was not all that dangerous, or he truly was a monster. And it was to this second hypothesis that I ever confidently clung.

Because he loved me, that creature, and to be loved by a monster is the best possible protection from the horrific world. Sure, he besmirched himself with heinous acts such as the killing of slugs or the skinning of rabbits, whose gory pelts he hung on tree branches without any concern for my tender age; but I was intelligent enough to understand that, to a monster, some concessions must be made. My grandfather tried to confound me, rationalizing the slaughter of mollusks with the necessity of preserving the lettuce, and the sacrificing of rabbits with the deliciousness of my grandmother's stews. But I knew that these were excuses, that the monster killed with pomp and pleasure, and that this alone counted, the barbarous satisfaction he obtained as executioner. Besides, to qualify him as a monster would have sufficed those disgusting gobs of spit, for which my grandfather's specious dialectic could find no justification.

And then, was there any knowing when he had been born, or where? What he had done before he started working for us? If he had relatives? Had anyone ever entered his home, if a home it was, that unknown space on the other side of a little door of grayish wood? Had anyone ever seen him dressed in anything other than that coverall, the same one throughout the decades? Could anyone say they had ever seen him go grocery shopping, or have goods delivered? And what did he eat? He drank a lot, evidently, but was there a single person in the whole town who could attest to a bottle going through that little door? And, finally, I needed a monster, and this was the deciding factor. Moreover, did he not handle that terrible poison unscathed?

Once broken up in water, the verdigris formed a dense paste, similar to the one confectioners used to twist about at old-time fairs as though fighting with a python. It had to remain in this state for a few days to "breathe," a verb that said all too much about the life of that thing. To this end, the bin was left dangerously open: I would go again and again into the woodshed to check on that mysterious respiratory activity, and as I contemplated the wondrous turquoise, I tried not to lean over it for fear of toxic exhalations, a fear validated by the little dead insects that bespeckled the color in continually increasing numbers.

When the time came, the man poured the paste into a large gritstone tub, whose presence meant the woodshed was occasionally called the laundry, with a transitivity that, while baffling for outsiders, signified for me the place's metamorphic and magical nature. Having added a good deal of water into the tub, he "mashed" it, meaning he stirred it with a long stick until the liquid became uniform. "Ye see, Michelín, be like mashin' p'lenta," he said; then he spat *into* the tub and, machinelike, continued to stir. Was it only a habit, or did that spit contain the necessary enzymes for the operation's success, like one of those secret ingredients on which every talented chef builds his fame? I never found out. Having obtained the desired result, his actions became incredibly quick: he needed to fill the tank before the mixture in the tub could "be breakin'"—that is, just as people mistakenly say in reference to mayonnaise, before the ingredients could separate. Then, after one final and more vigorous rotation of the stick, the artificer took a large copper tank and submerged it until full; he then closed the tank, securing the lid with two levers, and dried and wiped it with two different cloths so that the verdigris, as he had explained to me, wouldn't ruin the copper's shine; raising it high in the air, he shook it like the monstrous cocktail shaker of an even more monstrous barman, after which he attached two leather belts for shoulder straps and, like a backpack from the First World War, effectively stuck it to his backside. Thus laden, he hopped two or three times to better position it; then, removing with alacrity a cap screwed onto the lid, he twisted into the top of the tank the nut of a rubber tube, which had a long metallic tip on the opposite end—it, too, made of copper and identical in shape to a pastry syringe, but for the ringlike handle farther down, which recalled the one on a Winchester. At this point, I had already taken a few steps back, because I knew what was about to happen next: with the tube's syringe pointed into the air, the officiant pulled the ring toward him, causing the verdigris to spurt outward, first reluctantly and in oversized drops, then, at last, as a robust spray. Unrepeatable oaths came from the mouth of that ogre until the spurt was to his liking: whereupon, with all that copper on his back reminding me of the deep-sea divers of the *Nautilus*, he turned toward me and pretended to spray me, making a "psssss" sound, but a second after that he had already forgotten about me and was fully absorbed in his task.

Two hours later, the entire vineyard was spotted with turquoise splotches, so thick and concentrated as to tint at times an entire leaf or a half-bunch of grapes. "An' another verd'gris done, so," grumbled my man as he reentered the woodshed-laundry to wash off his instrument and empty the tub, which retained on its surface a turquoise incrustation I felt it was a crime to remove, but which was, nonetheless, routinely eliminated with a metal spatula and yet more water.

The verdigris! For years, I was convinced that this wondrous name was the natural sum of the grayish copper of the tank and the green of the vineyard; instead, it related only to the copper itself, due to the color it assumes when oxidized or, as I would discover as an adult, when it becomes copper acetate.

Looking at the verdigris-spotted vineyard, I was one day seized by a burning question: how was it possible that the man's coverall—onto which I had just seen droplets trickle down off the leaves with my own two eyes—had not become over time a composition of stains, rays, galaxies of that same color? Dirt and rabbit blood, yes; rust, motor grease too, lime, plaster; but not verdigris. Of course, verdigris is applied twice a year, whereas he had to tend to the garden, the animals, and the house every day: and yet . . . and yet at the very least he must have had more than one coverall, something that my mind simply couldn't accept, since it implied an embarrassing level of frivolity for a being such as him: multiple coveralls, yet all of them identical, just like the shoes of those English lords who have twelve pairs made at a time . . . And who washed away the verdigris? Did he do it himself, or did some woman in the town?

The answer, as cruel destiny would have it, came not long after, as though the sorrowful facts that merged therein had been conjured by my own questioning.

It was the beginning of August, when the soon-to-ripen grapes required their second coating of verdigris. As usual, my grandparents were shut up in some part of the house. The gate opens, and I see him: he should be cutting across the lawn toward the woodshed, but instead he goes the long way around, hugging the wall behind the fir trees. However, when he comes out into the open in front of the hayloft, he can no longer hide—hide, I mean, the extraordinary novelty of his beige-khaki coverall, that chromatic point which is more precisely hazelnut, and which I've never heard described by grandmothers and aunts as anything other than "a nice noisette." Dressed in that way, he looks like an English soldier, and with that tank on his back he'd make a perfect mine clearer. But soon he realizes I'm there and he turns around.

"Michelín?"

"That's me."

"Nothin' doin', Michelín."

"Why?"

"Now I make the verd'gris, righ'?"

"Yes."

"Then I spray it on 'em grapes, righ'?"

"Right."

"Righ' a blast'd thing!"

"Why?"

"Am I t' be sprayin' the verd'gris, an' meself all colored shite?"

"Really, it looks like a nice noisette to me . . ."

"Noisette me arse! Sure I spray the verd'gris, I do, but 'en? When I be gettin' home?"

He then explains to me: for two days, he has been desperately looking for his blue coveralls but he can't remember where he put them. And yet his home is small, you couldn't hide something in it if you tried . . . He therefore doesn't know what to think . . . Actually, he knows all too well and is terrified at the thought, for it is something that, sooner or later, befell all his ancestors like a curse.

"Michelín, I'm losin' me mem'ry, so."

Coupled with a tear welling up in one of his half-closed eyes, this sentence leaves me dumbstruck. He, meanwhile, doesn't give me time to respond and steals out of view, into the woodshed. For the first time, I don't follow him, leaving him to prepare the verdigris on his own.

Ancestors . . . So that man wasn't simply a natural product of nature, an unwitting drop in the ocean of living matter: instead, he knew an age-old story in which he played a part, his vision of the world not stopping at direct experiences but extending in depth and perspective . . . On one hand, this idea vexed me, because a monster with a family tree was ridiculous; on the other, it captivated me, because it granted an opportunity to dwell on the concept of hereditary maladies, a very dear concept to me, it being at the intersection of the themes of degeneration, affliction, and curses. Each son more monstrous than his father, but more monstrous than them all was the earliest forefather, capable of infecting all the generations to come . . . A story biblical and gothic at the same time, Darwinian and Lombrosian: I could say as much even at my young age, since gothic novels had been my very first bread and butter, I had read the Bible as well as *On the Origin of Species*, and, in terms of Lombroso, my father had sufficiently educated me the time I mustered the courage to ask him why, whenever he met someone he considered an imbecile (in other words, ninety-nine percent of the human race), he'd walk away from the encounter muttering that name, the sound of which brought to my mind the image of a lumbering troll. I had even read *Of Mice and Men*, immediately bestowing on Lennie the appearance of my rabbit farmer, and you could say that this completed the picture.

So, his hereditary malady was of an amnestic nature, and its discovery, or at least its confession, was linked to his unlocatable blue coveralls. Who could say how many other signs had already appeared to him before he decided to take that leap. Yes, a true leap, because sharing that secret with a young boy was, for that strong-limbed man, clearly tantamount to making a cry for help— no, more: to putting his life in that boy's hands. I told myself that if he had turned to me, he must truly be alone, although I was also flattered by the idea that he had intuited in me the most fraternal and congenial spirit in the whole town. Was I not perhaps a connoisseur of monsters, willing with every fiber of my being to make friends with them, to understand them, to love them?

The day after that conversation, he appeared once again in his blue coverall; apparently his amnesia hadn't lasted long. I ran over to congratulate him, but before I even reached him I realized how mistaken I was. He was paler than I had ever seen him, and against that pallor the purple of his birthmark and his web of veins stood out with graphic mercilessness. Most importantly, he didn't spit right after coming through the gate, a ritual that for years had obligated me to exit at a slant in order to avoid the patch of contaminated grass.

"Michelín," he said, with the voice of a man on the brink of tears.

"Yes?"

"Michelín—meself, wha's the name on me?"

I did not want to believe that his malady could have galloped at such a pace.

"Me name, blast it, wha' the blazes 'm I called?"

"Felice."

"Felís . . . me?"

"Yes, Felice."

"Fancy tha', an' I thinkin' me name were Danilo . . ."

"And why Danilo, exactly?"

"Oh 'cause o' 'em posters all o'er, Danilo Goretti an' his ban', t'nigh' at Bress de Béder an' the morra at Germignaga."

That near-chameleonlike passivity immediately gave me an idea. We needed to find something—something concrete and objective—that could remind him, when necessary, of a forgotten word or idea. Felice, felicity . . . but felicity was complex and abstract (if it existed at all). We needed something more obvious and immediate, something that would spark an automatic association through sound too, a play on words . . . Here, my experience as a boredom-fueled solver of old, yellowed crossword puzzles came to my aid with the most fitting item in the dictionary and in the entire vegetable kingdom: fleece. The "fleece flower," just one example of the ineradicable knotweed species that plagued horticulturists like my monster more than anything. And so, without really thinking about what I was doing, I ran behind the larch, where there was an enormous quantity of knotweed, picked a stem, and brought it to him.

"Stick this to your wall next to your bed, so that when you wake up and you've forgotten your name, you can look at it and be reminded: it's exactly how you say your own name, if you just remove the 'e.'"

"A 'e' . . ."

"Yes. Fleece, Felís!"

"T' guess this 'ere dirty weed be any use ye'd be wantin' a sorc'ress . . ."

"So you pretend that the fleece is your sorceress. You ask her a question and she'll answer you. She'll answer only you. Only for you does her message carry any meaning."

"A somethin' jus' for me, ye says?"

"Exactly, for you and you alone."

"Cripes—fleeces!"

"In exchange, though, you have to promise me that you'll stop killing slugs."

"But they're Frensh, 'em rott'n buggers o' slugs."

"I know, but they're innocent little creatures all the same."

"Inn'cent me arse, an' all the lettuce they're after eatin'!"

"Lettuce won't help you, but the fleece will."

And with this sentence uttered in bad faith, I obtained immunity for all those iridescently slimy gastropods. I obtained it for a week, until one morning, at my grandmother's request, I went into the garden to pick some chicory. Everywhere, amid the heads of lettuce, languished the halved cadavers of red slugs. Two days earlier there had been a long storm, due to which the little creatures must have come out into the open in droves. But why that mass slaughter? Why so much fury, after our agreement? Some of them had been struck by the spade right where they were, so that along with their bodies, the heads of lettuce on which they crawled had likewise been chopped in two; others displayed imprecise wounds, as though, in his rage, Felice had lost his flawless aim.

I waited for him to show himself, quivering with indignation, but when he did appear he was more indignant than I.

"Bugger off ta hell wi' yer fleeces!" he said, and he kept on walking toward the woodshed, without adding another word.

"But you promised! The slugs!" I shouted, as I ran after him.

"Ay, a promise . . . an' 'f I were forgettin' abou' tha' promise, me lad? Can be forgettin' ev'rythin', don' ye know?" and he guffawed, showing his seven blackened teeth. So, he was even going to make a joke of it!

"You didn't forget. You promised and you remembered!" I insisted.

"Ay, but tha' stinkin' weed were makin' a cod outa me."

"Why? You forgot your name again?"

"Know me name, don' need a plant for tha'! 'Twere the jacks I weren't findin' no!"

"The jacks?"

"Woke th' other day havin' to take a piss, but a piss the like o' . . . An' like I says, am not knowin' where's the jacks! Go lookin' ev'rywhere, an' I seein' yer fleece there 'tached to the wall an' sayin' help me, an' takin' 'way the 'e' an' grabbin' 't off the wall an' puttin' it back like, but o' the jacks not a peep out 'f it, an' I searshin' an' searshin' till I piss meself—blast'd feckin' filt'!"

"But your toilet isn't inside, you've got your outhouse! How have you managed since?"

He squinted his eyes, smiling with a knowing air: "Went on yeez's lawn so—piss an' shite!" and he laughed once more.

"Felice, try to understand: the fleece was for your name; for the bathroom you'll need something else."

"Oh blazes, an' if t'morra I forgeh where the knife be I'm needin' another whassit for me knife?"

"That's right, for each thing its own helper."

I didn't know, with those words, what road I was setting out on.

The following period inflicted a frightening acceleration in the development of Felice's malady. Soon enough, not a day would go by without the addition of another mental gap: it was as though the world was, little by little, growing smaller around him, losing pieces of itself, pieces that were things, that were words, places, memories. Sometimes he knew what was being referred to but simply couldn't remember its name: in this way, lettuce became tender salad, endive bitter salad, and chicory even more bitter salad. Sometimes he managed to hold on to the name but only as a meaningless utterance, and he would ask me what a spade was, or what the meaning was of that "blast it" which was continually forming in his mouth. Other times he retained both thing and word but, as with his toilet, no longer knew how to locate it. In terms of his memories, they were surely disappearing at a devastating rate, because for every erasure that he noticed there must have been many others that, by the very virtue of the memory having vanished, left no sign and inspired no suspicion. Poor Felice! I thought of him as the opposite of Condillac's statue, as he went from complete individual (albeit a monstrous one) to mere simulacrum of a man, his speech deteriorating just as quickly as his mind. It was clear that the course of his illness was irreversible; but I could help him to make do, and to keep the symptoms hidden from others, above all from my grandfather, who would not have thought twice before firing him as pitilessly as a landowner in a Dickens novel. He, for that matter, clung to me with so much trust that I could not shirk my responsibility—and besides, has there ever been anything more irresistible than a monster who asks you for help?

Thus, in a short span of time, his little hovel, where I had finally been admitted, became filled with memento-signs which, once he'd understood the general apparatus, he turned to for help, and almost always successfully. *Almost* always: because—and it was a real shame, too—every so often he would lose all recollection of the right pairing despite only a short time having elapsed, and would interrogate a sign that concerned something else entirely. And another curious phenomenon presented itself when, forgetting the sign's preliminary function but not its meaning, he tended to substitute it directly for what it signified, investing it with *all* the meaning. As a result, he told me one day that he was called "the fleece man," whereas another day he informed me, while running to his house, that he had to go "t' 'em signs"—it took me a little while to understand that what he had in mind were the two black arrow signs that I had drawn, one inside his home and one outside on the railed-in walkway, to point him to the toilet.

Mix-ups of this sort were sooner or later going to arouse my grandfather's suspicion. The first time was when Felice asked him if he needed to plant more milk: only three days prior, to help him remember the word for lettuce, I had suggested he think of "lactose," adding that it was not an arbitrary association, since the word "lettuce" came precisely from the milky fluid that oozes out of it when you slice the head. I also remember being surprised on that occasion by how he intuited the vertiginous transitivity that would eventually undermine the foundations of the whole system: "Then unripe figs is la'tose, an' the bress o' lasses an' she-goats an' pussycats, but ye can't be thinkin' always o' milk, blast it!"

"No, you know how it works by now: for each thing, one other thing . . . For example, if you've forgotten the word for breasts, think of chicken breasts . . ."

"Ay, an' for pussycat, think o' pussy!"

Here he was ready to let out a guffaw; but he stopped just after beginning to grin and, his facial muscles frozen, stood still with a rapt look in his eyes. Once again, he was about to surprise me.

"Or 's it tha' 'f I forgeh pussy, I've to be thinkin' o' pussycat?"

"One or the other, really . . . Like an alliance between two friends: when one is in need, the other helps."

"Y'are a quick one, sure. An' if I forgeh 't all, pussycat an' pussy, chicken bress an' lasses' bress, wha' then?"

"Look . . . I think certain fundamental things are impossible to forget . . . milk, for example . . . or that . . . that other thing that you said . . ."

"But I'm on'y after forgettin' me name! An' tell me there were e'er a thing more 'portant than a fella's own name!"

"That . . . that other thing. It seems pretty important to me too."

"Lis'n 'ere lad, wha' age's ye?"

"Thirteen and a half."

"An' a' thirteen t' be talkin' so? But d'ye ev'n know wha' pussy be?"

"No, I mean yes, I've heard about it . . ."

"Ah! Me who knowed it 's needin' ye who hasn't to 'member wha' it be like!"

"Not what it's like, because I wouldn't know how to tell you that; just what it's called. For that, the image of a pussycat might come in handy."

"An' if I were wantin' to know wha' 'twere like, insi' an' out?"

"Well, then you have to recover your memories, and remember the women you've been with, their names . . . You're still able to do that, right?"

"Bah! Firs' lass I made love wi' were called Marisa . . ."

"And then?"

"'Member her arse on'y, such a big arse, like, an' tha' she was dark-haired. An' no more."

"And were there others?"

"Eh, others! Tree or four, wha' d'ye think now?"

"But, so, what about the . . . pussy?"

"Oh, a gran' thing, for 'em tha' understan's it . . . Me? Never understant nothin'."

"But you must remember something."

"Dunno . . . le' me think . . . I were there wi' me prick out . . . Eh, but can I be sayin' the like an' ye jus' a wee 'un?"

"You can . . . you must!"

"Ach, fine! I were there, an' Jen'vieve lyin' there wi' her legs op'n'd . . . her legs op'n'd . . ."

"And then?"

"An' then nothin'! Don't 'member a damn bleedin' thing for chrissake!"

"So I guessed it, when I said the pussycat would come in handy . . ."

"Guessed it, guessed it—happy? An' wha' could a fella be doin' wi' pussy now, anyway . . . Meself's too ould, an' yerself, y'are too young."

We spun around in sterile discussions such as this one, which had something academic to them. Could things have gone any differently, for that matter, between a young boy with no experience of life and a semiliterate old man? But there was his disease—no, his hereditary curse—and I realized the problem preoccupied him, almost enchanted him. So, at the risk of being a know-it-all, I had no choice but to continue with my maieutic maneuvers.

I started to assign him homework. Every evening, while he watered the garden, an activity that took more than an hour, I tested him. My questions concerned both things he had forgotten, for which I had supplied him with a like number of mental or material mementos, and random other things in order to gauge the progression of his illness. In terms of the first category, I quickly realized that material aids were far more fruitful than mental ones, so much so that I ended up giving him objects of very limited size that he could carry constantly on his person, in the capacious pockets of his coveralls. My tests thus took the form of a haphazard search through those pockets.

"So, what's the name of this town?"

While holding the hose in his right hand and aiming the water at the lettuce, he dug with his left in side pockets and breast pockets stuffed with objects. He pulled out a little plastic elephant, considered it for a few seconds, but then put it back in its place, dug some more and pulled out a Panini card, looked at me as if awaiting some confirmation, but I shook my head, the player being Paride Tumburus; then he started to panic under the pressure and pulled out three or four objects at a time, while I, in my disapproval, didn't even shake my head . . . In the end he found the right object: one of my Mercury toy cars, an American racing model with NASCAR written on the side, and ... "Nasca!" he shouted, and in that shout converged his own origins and the future, that town in the Varesotto and the far-off land of opportunity. As for my own name, I had given him a plastic rooster, because when I was little he always used to sing me the song "San Michele Had a Rooster." This expedient, however, risked disastrous consequences, because on the day he decided to kill our rooster, he went to my grandfather and announced that he had murdered me. "I done in Michelín," he told him, his hands dripping with blood—since, generally speaking, women break the necks of chickens while men decapitate them—and luckily my grandfather had already become a bit deaf and absentminded due to his age, because otherwise I don't know what might have happened.

In any event, unfortunate setbacks such as these emerged continuously. One day I saw him arrive looking puffed up, as though his clothes had been stuffed with straw or pumped full of compressed air, his pockets stretched to the point that they appeared a lighter blue than the rest of his coverall.

"What did you do?"

"Heehee ... shhh ... don' go tellin' nobody, but I be full o' women," and as he said this, onto the grass he emptied large tufts of what looked like cat fur, which he had crammed into his pockets like the pubic hair of so many odalisques; and—a fact that moved and disturbed me at the same time—in the middle of one of those tufts was my little plastic rooster, because "wi' all 'em women, I were wantin' me Michelín t' 'ave some o' the fun."

Gripped by this fever, he tended to invest any given thing with other meanings, as if the world, which until recently had been shrinking all around him, had started to expand again: a medieval man in his symbolism, an ancient man in his pan-symbolism, he was growing before my very eyes, a living demonstration of how much greater nature is than history. I realized this when he came to inspect our roof, which since time immemorial had leaked whenever it rained. To reach the attic crawlspace, he had to go up two flights of stairs, and there was not a single thing, during our ascent, that did not speak to him of something else.

"The step," he began, placing his boot on the first stone step, "be real useful, see, 'cause it tells ye t' be takin' another step after: else ye'd be rollin' down the like 'f a sausage."

"I suppose so . . ." I replied, feeling incredibly stupid.

On the wall along the first flight of stairs were hung prints depicting mythological subjects. Walking past them, without even looking, he stated, "Paintin's is useful to the rich for to remin' 'em they're rich." Struck by this observation halfway between Lukács and Adorno, I was soon called back downward by the combined similitude that followed: "Be the same for beards, 'cause in the mornin' y'are needin' somethin' tha' tells ye if y'are a fella or a lass." Along the second flight were two other prints covered in water stains. "Sure the wet remin's us wha' we's came for: the roof!" he exclaimed, quite satisfied with himself; but on the next landing he was left speechless in front of a drying rack that had been brought inside due to the bad weather. I motioned to him to keep going, but he blocked me with his arm: evidently he didn't want to leave anything without its own special gloss. Actually, from his behavior it seemed that coming to our house that day was a kind of exam for him.

"This 'ere be a rack, sure 'nough . . . an' wi' tree draw's, four socks . . . a shirt . . . blazes but I amn't gettin' it! An' then y'ave yer clo'espins, one, two, tree, four . . . nine . . . seven pins, ay! Need t' be doin' som'in' 'portant on the sevent' o' the mont'? Don' think so . . . Hol' on! Eight's the pins so they are, 'ere's one 'tached to the side, eight . . . Ah! Th' eight's when am needin' to get the dole a' the pos' office."

He was so convinced, I didn't have the heart to tell him that with those clothes he could have similarly arrived at any possible conclusion by taking into consideration their shape and color, their arrangement, or the various members of the family to whom they belonged, not to mention by conducting any number of arithmetic operations with the pins themselves. I didn't have the heart to tell him, but we had just started walking up the steps again when he confronted the demon of desemanticization all on his own.

"But . . . lis'n, 'em pins's sof' on their en's, righ'?"

"Of course."

"So why call 'em pins? An' to think 'f it, 'em thingsits in lasses' hair is called pins too . . ."

"Yes, but clothespins are pins because they pin things down, I think, not because they have sharp ends that give you a pin-prick . . ."

"Usin' the same word for what a lass be puttin' in her hair an' for wha's goin' on her draw's, sure 't seems mighty quare to me . . ."

"Felice, you don't have to try to make everything add up, otherwise you'll go crazy. There are things that don't need to interest us. You just stick to what you've established and what will come in handy for you." I knew that the question of arbitrariness would produce frightening cracks in the system, and I wasn't mistaken.

"But if I choose it meself, the meanin', I can also be gettin' it wrong, no?"

"No, because we don't need to worry about the history of things and words; we just need to use them at our own convenience."

"Well 'en, why for to 'member me name's Felís was ye givin' me a plant?"

"Because we need something that reminds you of the thing you have to remember, but it all depends on you. If someone named Riccardo sees a fleece flower, it's not like it'll make him remember *his* name, right?"

He looked perplexed and inexpressive, but I knew that the mental effort he was making was equal to Bacon's when he conceived the *Novum Organum*.

"Plants is called so 'cause y'ave to plant 'em in the groun', an' ye don' need to call yerself Felís t' be gettin' that."

"Wrong, because plants don't just grow where we plant them, but all over in nature. Don't get too wrapped up in similar sounds or in every word with multiple meanings."

"But 'twas yerself says soun's 'd be remin'in' me o' things! Bugger ta hell but I don' understan' a damn bleedin' thing!"

"You can associate sounds and words any way you like. You can associate anything the way you like, so long as it works."

A half hour later, while he was in the crawlspace from the waist up and I was holding the ladder steady, he put another question to me. With a shudder, I wondered if his brain had been working in this manner from the moment I had handed him that weed.

"Michelín?"

His voice reached me from the ceiling hatch, now taken up almost entirely by his hips. If I looked up, I saw his enormous behind swathed in faded blue.

"Yes?"

"Takin' shites—t'ain't pretty, but it be somethin' 'portant like, 'cause if a person don't shite, they burs'."

"I can't argue with you there . . ."

"An' so the jacks be 'portant too, but less, 'cause a body can go in a field, but sure it be 'portant all th' same. An' so I were needin' signs a' me home, 'cause in 'em moments y'aven't time to be playin' wi' letters an' names, no: jus' 'op to an' off ye go!"

His *an' so*s and *'cause*s had the peremptory and indisputable value of an Aristotelian *ergo*, but I knew they were building to an objection.

"But losin' yer mem'ry ain't jus' forgettin' things, no—'t also be forgettin' mem'ries, an' mem'ries's more 'portant than yer jacks..."

I kept quiet, though whether out of respect or cowardice, I can't say.

"Me da, for 'xample, I don' know wha' face he had on 'im, y'understan'? His face, Michelín, the face o' me da!"

He, too, stopped speaking for a moment, while he scraped at the underside of the roof tiles with a crowbar. Then he began again, even more agitated than before. "But for faces ye can't be puttin' signs in yer mem'ry, blast it—ye can't be, no! An' so?"

"Felice, the arrows are only for pointing to a specific place in reality."

"An' ain't me da real?"

"Yes, but he's dead, he's no longer anywhere, or he's everywhere essentially, he's in your head..."

"An' me head, t'ain't real?"

"Yes, but the things inside it are like ghosts: they're inside it but they're bodiless, they're placeless, so you have to choose the right aids in order to find them again."

"More 'an fin'in' 'em, keepin' 'em still, 'cause a' times he comes back to me as clear as the day, me da, but when he wants it so, an' when I tries keepin' 'im—s'long!—an' he's lef' me."

When he came back down, whacking the dust from his coverall, I took another step down that incredibly risky road.

"Listen, this year in school we read a story taken from the life of a famous sculptor named Benvenuto Cellini. The story was titled 'An Instructive Salamander.' You'll have seen tons of salamanders, right? Well, in those days, hundreds of years ago, there were very few, and, most importantly, people believed back then that they fed on fire and that flames couldn't burn them . . . One day, when he's about five years old, little Benvenuto is called by his father to come right away to the lit fireplace. 'Look!' his father says, pointing at the salamander in the fire, and he gives him a terrible slap in the face; then, while his son is crying, he explains to him that since he risked forgetting that extraordinary event at his young age, he had no choice but to slap him so that the episode would stay etched in his mind for the rest of his life . . . Do you understand? That inexplicable and unfair wallop was the safe in which the memory was preserved, to the extent that half a century later Benvenuto began his autobiography precisely with that salamander."

"But weren't there the danger tha' wi' ev'ry slap Benvenu'd be 'memb'rin' sal'manders?"

"Maybe, but either way, it worked. Therefore, the next time your father's face comes back to you, you should do something like that to yourself."

"A big clatter, like?"

"No, if you gave it to yourself, you wouldn't feel the mortification and shock that Benvenuto experienced. You'd need something stronger . . ."

"Ay, like a nail?"

"Are you crazy?"

"Now lookit, me da . . . me da's 'portant." He started to cry softly, a sight I couldn't bear.

"Dads are important for everyone, Felice."

"But more 'portant for me, y'understan'? More, I says, damn an' blast it ta bleedin' hell!"

Why did a father have to be more important for him than for anyone else? Could I have answered with the obvious assertion that, for better or worse, every male sees his own father as the most important figure in the world? No, I couldn't. And I couldn't because I had gleaned an analogical nuance in his objection: he knew full well that everyone has his own father, who's irreplaceable for that individual; what he was telling me was that, proportionally, due to the course his life had taken, a father figure—or rather, the memory of such a figure—carried a greater weight than in many other lives, perhaps even in my own . . .

I am in his home, which consists of a single room and a little balcony facing our property. On the opposite side is the front door, which, as we already know, leads to the outhouse at the end of the walkway; an outhouse that, thankfully, Felice does not have to share with anyone else, the other sections and would-be apartments of the house being used as sheds, haylofts, and storage rooms.

On the walls, no free space any bigger than a postcard remains: everywhere has gradually been overrun by objects and signs drawn on paper, when not by symbols traced directly onto the plaster. Anyone walking into that room would have the impression of a random and compulsive clutter, as though owing to a kind of *horror vacui*: only the two of us know how much reflection has actually gone into every single element, and how agonizing the struggle with the scarcity of available space has been. The first mementos were suggested by me: from the fateful fleece flower and the two famous lavatory arrows, to the two-dimensional development of a milk carton with the word "lactose" circled on it to remind him of the word for lettuce; from the model car recalling the name of the town, to the little rooster that pointed to my own name; from a postcard depicting the aurora borealis, intended to remind him that his father's name was Aurelio, to a plush feline that, in the absence of the thing itself, could at least remind him of the word for it, to an ear of barley that, should we so desire, could come in handy for having some barley water, and so on. But everything else was his, in the sense that, after nailing and gluing twenty or so objects to his walls, he decided to forge ahead on his own. The first few times, I observed him and had to correct him in spite of myself, because his inclination was to have the thing correspond to the thing, the *same* thing: he had been to the Festa dell'Unità at Porto Valtravaglia and had liked the sausages? The next day one of those sausages, still greasy though already shriveled, was there on display, nailed to his wall.

"But that's not the way mnemonics work!" I blurted out, imprudently.

"Memonics me arse! Y'arc the one's bangin' on abou' signs 'ere an' signs there! An' so I wanta know why a sausage ain't the righ' way t' be 'memb'rin' sausage!"

"Because if you need to bring back to mind a sausage, that means that in that moment you no longer know what a sausage is, and so even if you see it hanging on the wall it will still mean nothing to you, nothing at all! Or else you'll know what a sausage is but not what it's called, and having it on the wall won't help you then either."

"An' so?"

"And so you need something indirect, something that circumvents the problem and leads you to the sausage by taking you down a path that you can't even imagine."

"An' do they be teachin' ye this in school, Michelín?"

"Of course not! Or maybe . . . And even if they did, would it bother you?"

"Talkin' wi' ye, I feel like I understan' it all, 'en next time, like I don' understan' a thing."

"That's normal for a student. And now you're studying how not to lose your memory."

"Ach, fine! Tell me yerself wha' I should a' been puttin' on me wall 'stead o' sausage."

"Setting aside that after a little while a sausage goes bad and becomes full of maggots and larvae, if you wanted to remember how much you enjoyed it, you could have put up a hammer and sickle."

"Hammer an' sickle? I'm no Comm'nis'!"

"But you go to the fairs organized by the Communist Party, and you enjoy them."

"When there's food t' eat, y'are not both'rin' wi' pol'tics."

"Great, for you the hammer and sickle is a sausage and only a sausage—so put it up."

I then saw that splotched and misshapen creature take a burnt piece of wood from the fireplace and use it to draw a shoddy hammer and sickle on his bedroom wall. While he was at work, I thought of the ugly and bureaucratic face of the party leader Togliatti, because faces are faces and they don't lie, and if anyone had a Christian Democrat face, it was actually Togliatti. When I then asked my monster if the names Palmiro or Alcide meant anything to him, he said no; and when he asked, guiltily, if that was a bad thing and if he had to stick something to the wall to remember them, I told him that it wasn't necessary, and that really he should consider his ignorance vis-à-vis those two exotic names a blessing.

"Garibaldi, on the other hand, now he was a great man. You know who Garibaldi was?"

"The hero o' two worl's!"

"Right, so as far as politics is concerned, let's just make do with Garibaldi, agreed?"

"Agree! An' they ev'n pluggin' 'im in the leg, th' poor Gar'baldi!"

And so we both agreed to be Garibaldians, and the festering sausage was replaced by the hammer and sickle. Monsters I could tolerate to the farthest limits of my imagination—but not Christian Democrat monsters. It was 1969: I was in love with the singer Nada, but wore myself out thinking of Sylvie Vartan; in Madrid, Milan beat Cruyff's Ajax four–one with three goals from Prati, and would soon go on to win the Intercontinental Cup in a battle with Estudiantes, a match that would forever leave me with the heroic image of the swollen eye of Néstor Combin, called "La Foudre." But more than anything, 1969 was the year of the monster.

A monster who, the day after our last conversation, amazed me with two solutions of his own invention. He had, in the interim, replaced the drawing of the hammer and sickle with a real hammer and a real sickle, nailed through the handles and thus affixed to the wall: only a year earlier, my father had exhibited something similar at the Milan Triennale. Then, since the question of the sausage had evidently continued to preoccupy him, he had put up a magazine cutout with a picture of Ada Roe, the oldest woman in the world, and glued above it an empty tomato sauce can.

"And this means?"

"Sauce, age: sausage!"

"You see the kind of progress you're making? Well done!"

"An' so, seein' 'ow I done, can I be killin' two or tree slugs?"

"No, a deal's a deal."

"But on'y 'em righ' Frensh buggers!"

"No, they're slugs all the same. And besides, why do you hate the French ones? The Italian ones eat your vegetables too!"

"'F one's to be eatin' 'em, 'tween the two I ra'er 't be our own brothers, an' . . . an' they've somethin' to do wi' me da, 'em Frensh."

"The Italian slugs are our brothers?! What in the world are you saying? All animals are our brothers, all of them! And do you really believe these red slugs regularly journey here from France? Don't you understand that they were born here, and that if they ever did come from France, they're Italian by now? The potato came from America, and yet people have been growing it in Italy for centuries . . ."

"Not me, be food for Krauts."

"But you drink coffee, don't you?"

"Not on yer life, no. Blacks do be drinkin' it."

"Arabs aren't Black."

"Same thing, like!"

"Well, what do you eat, what do you drink? Only Italian stuff? You realize that autarky is long gone?"

"Ne'er heard 'f o'tarky. I like 'em red an' black fizzy drinks, or'ngeade, lem'n soda, lem'nade, but more 'an anythin' I like wine."

"You sound like you're in the ranks of the Alpini."

"An' so? Y'ave somethin' 'gainst th' Alpini?"

"No, not at all, but . . . why did you say the French have something to do with your father?"

"Ah, boyo! Ye forgeh tha' I were losin' me mem'ry?"

"So you no longer know what the French have to do with anything . . ."

"I don' 'member nothin' abou' me da—would ye get tha' int' yer head now?"

"But it seems to me that you don't remember anything about your mother either, or about the rest of your family for that matter, seeing as you've never been able to tell me if you were an only child or if you had brothers or sisters, or if those siblings are still alive, or where they live, what they do. You don't remember a single thing about all that, but it doesn't seem to me that it ever bothered you very much. Your father, on the other hand, obsesses you, he comes up all the time when you talk, and now we find out that he's even somehow the cause of your war with the French slugs!"

"Stinkin' Frensh!"

"All nationalities stink, if you only consider their worst aspects."

"Michelín."

Whenever he addressed me in this abrupt manner, without any connection to what had just been said, I knew he was about to bring up something important, something painful that he had long kept to himself.

"Yes?"

"Wha's me age, d'ye think?"

"Fifty-something . . . fifty-eight, sixty at most. Why?"

"Firs', we've t' be fin'in' ou' me age, an' sec'nd, t' be settlin' if me da migh' still be 'live or no."

"Still alive?"

I asked my grandfather how long Felice had worked for us: it turned out that, when they had bought the house, he was theoretically already part of it, and that the previous owner, a Russian man named Kropoff, recommended him as an honest and able worker, who had "always" been in his service. At that time, the valuable factotum must have already been at least forty or so years old, so my idea that he was now almost sixty was credible. But what did "always" mean? Since he was old enough to work, or since he was taken in as a foundling? The second scenario could explain why no one in town, including the man in question, knew his last name. A visit to the parish priest wasn't much help, because Felice didn't appear in any of the birth records, a fact that in turn could mean two things: either he wasn't born in Nasca, or his birth had occurred under conditions of such great scandal and secrecy as to have never officially taken place. The cover granted by the Kropoffs, in the latter case, would have been crucial, but why would a family of Russian nobles fleeing the motherland at the outbreak of the revolution go through that trouble, if not to cover up the affair of one of their own descendants with a commoner? With a commoner who was almost certainly working for them as a maidservant, since it had apparently been possible to keep the pregnancy hidden within the walls of their house. Of *that* house—my own! I imagined what the décor had been like, what faces the czarists had, and I realized that this, too, was strange: that such an important family hadn't left any trace of itself, not a portrait, not a memory in the minds of the town's oldest inhabitants. That they might have never set foot beyond their front gate was plausible, given the paranoia that led escapees to see Stalin's spies everywhere; but that they wouldn't have left in the house so much as a teaspoon with a K on the handle seemed truly peculiar. Especially since, as my grandfather informed me, the sale of the house had taken place in no time at all, as though the Kropoffs had been in a great hurry to disappear. Actually, the day my grandparents came to Nasca for the property to be officially handed over, the Kropoffs had already moved out without leaving a new address, and the only one who remained to represent them was Felice. I asked my grandfather if he had given the impression of a man who had been left behind, but he replied that, besides for his extraordinary ugliness, he had made no impression whatsoever. My grandmother was even a little scared of him, especially when he laughed, opening wide his huge mouth and revealing those few, already rotten teeth. As for me, all that I remember from the early days is that I associated that man with purple: the purple of his winish birthmark, the purple of his drowned man's lips, the purple veins that decorated his nose, the purple under his nails after the grape harvest. Only several years later, when I was allowed to keep him company as he worked, did his color become verdigris, a change that, like an alchemical miracle, made him suddenly appear less ugly.

Naturally, I had spoken to him about all these vicissitudes on multiple occasions, but to no avail. Not only did he remember nothing of his mother, he even claimed she had never existed. In response to my objection that this was technically impossible, he would shrink down into his shoulders, pushing out his lips as if to reply, "Who can say?" When presented with another objection, namely that he didn't remember anything about his father either, though he not only didn't doubt his existence but, on the contrary, considered him fundamental to his life, he would respond in one of two ways: either by pointing to the evidence of the first name Aurelio—as though it could not possibly have been another mistake or instance of outright paramnesia—or with the old story of the French slugs, against which Aurelio seemed to have fought a full-fledged crusade. Or maybe he alone was fighting a crusade, in order to avenge his father for an affront suffered at the hands of a Frenchman . . . Russians . . . Frenchmen . . . affronts and revenge . . . I was obsessed with Pushkin's duel with the vile d'Anthès, but could such legendary and golden stories—stories that now truly belonged to literature, and to an old literature at that—could they really have something in common with the Varesotto philistine, with the municipality of Castelveccana located between Laveno and Luino, with that land of gardeners and nurserymen? And furthermore . . . going down that literary rabbit hole . . . if little Felice really was the son of one of the Kropoffs' maidservants, and if the family had deemed it unsuitable to give him their last name, then he inevitably would have grown up with his mother, in the cramped servants' quarters and in the kitchen, without any opportunity to approach his father, who he probably didn't know was his father in the first place. Whether this man lived in Nasca with the other Kropoffs or had gone off on his own, one naturally had to imagine that his refusal to recognize the child had been total, and that the poor servant girl had been sworn to the strictest silence. Why, then? Why this indistinct memory of an absent father, while his present mother had faded into complete oblivion? It was illogical, nonsensical.

I tried to broach the topic from another angle:

"Felice, what's the first job you remember doing?"

"Firs' job? Peelin' spuds."

"Any other jobs?"

"Gettin' firewood, givin' feed to the chick'ns, carryin' up the hay, changin' the gas tanks, c'lectin' the grape harves', pullin' weeds, 'djustin' tiles, makin' lime mortar, sprayin' verd'gris . . ."

"Yes, but those are tasks that you started to do over time, when you were older. I mean the very first job, when you were just a child."

"Peelin' spuds."

"And were there any women with you?"

"Women? Don' think so."

"But there must have been someone there who gave you the potatoes, someone who told you how many to peel, someone who'd then cook them. You weren't always on your own in the kitchen, right?"

"Ay, seems I were always in the kitch'n on me own, me an' 'em spuds."

Charles Dickens—an amateur! But could it really be true? For example, could Aurelio have been the name of a Russian nobleman? I rather doubted it. Maybe that's where we needed to start, with the name.

Given that Felice could not positively remember a single time he had addressed his father by the name Aurelio—given that he was in fact unable to regain even the vaguest notion of the man—I had to proceed by formal and associative means. I invited him to close his eyes and to concentrate on the word "Aurelio," and then to tell me what came to mind. The first thing was obviously the postcard with the aurora borealis, but I was the one responsible for that, making it an element of no value. I insisted he try again: this time, he squeezed his eyes shut as children do when they want to convey a high degree of concentration. He pursed his lips too, whitening the purple. Then he spoke.

"A vess'l, for seafarin'."

Though my interlocutor was many years older than I was, something told me that *vessel* was even older, the kind of word our grandparents and great-grandparents might have used . . . Why hadn't he said *ship*, or *boat*?

"Think about it carefully: a ship, or a vessel?" I slyly asked.

"Vess'l, 'f I a'ready says vess'l!"

So it was the word, not the thing . . . And on Lake Maggiore of all places, where there was nothing more than the Laveno–Intra ferry . . .

"Felice, do you know the children's game that goes, 'A vessel has arrived, nice and full of . . .'"

He shook his head. "Ach, some game tha' . . ."

Now it was my turn to focus. Vessel . . . vessel . . . where could he have heard that word, why had it popped into his head? But of course! I should have thought of it sooner! "Santa Lucia Luntana," that heartrending song!

"'The vessels are leaving, for faraway lands . . .' Does that ring a bell?"

I saw him stiffen, as though growing suspicious: I had struck a nerve. He shook his head again.

"Try to remember, make an effort! You must have heard it."

"Now I'm after tellin' ye no . . ."

Suddenly, I remembered that years earlier, for their silver wedding anniversary, my uncle had given my grandparents a box set of the best Neapolitan songs, and this only because my grandfather regarded the song "Santa Lucia" and their engagement as one and the same. In no time at all, I had run to the library, found the His Master's Voice set and the disk with the desired song, descended to the living room, and, taking advantage of my grandparents' absence, turned on the gramophone. Felice, once summoned, listened solemnly, holding his cap in his hands.

"So?" I asked him once the song had ended.

He hesitated, then asked to hear it again. And while he listened to it a second time, I saw the singer's name on the cover. "Roberto Murolo and others," was written on the box set, and the great Murolo in fact sang fourteen of the fifteen songs on that disc. All except "Santa Lucía," which was sung by Aurelio Fierro.

His father's name, therefore, was nothing but the result of a song, a fact that pulled that dubious parent back into an even murkier realm of shadows.

"Felice, listen to me, you heard this song once, maybe on this very record, it moved you and left a lasting impression, and when you found out that it was sung by someone named Aurelio, that name made just as big an impression and stayed stuck in some part of your memory. Then, when you started not remembering things anymore and went searching for your father's name, you stopped at the first name that you found inside yourself."

"An' so?"

"And so your father wasn't named Aurelio."

"Ye sure?"

"Sure."

"Wha' a shame . . . wha' a shame . . ." And again he was ready to cry.

"It mattered a lot to you that he was named Aurelio?"

"T'ain't that . . . but . . . a singer from Naples, 'ow shameful, like!"

"Now, you listen to me. If you want the two of us to get along, you have to stop saying things like that, got it?"

"Ah sure, but . . ." He paused in the throes of profound torment. "But . . . then we can't be discov'rin' me da were a bleedin' south'ner, righ'?"

"I don't think so, but you never know . . . Do you want to find out? Well, then you have to be prepared for anything. Besides, be honest, have songs as beautiful as this one ever been written in the Varesotto? The way I see it, if you discovered that your father was from Mergellina, you'd only have reasons to celebrate."

"Dunno a thing abou' Neapolity tunes."

"But you knew 'Santa Lucia.'"

"Michelín."

"Yes?"

"I know somethin' no one knows."

"Well, go ahead and tell me then."

"Not ev'n yer granda knows it."

"Even better."

"On the side o' yeez's haylof', up 'bove, there be a room."

"I know, the one full of tools, where I've never been allowed to go."

"Ay, an' wha' be a' the back wall there?"

"The pieces of a dismantled bed."

"An' behint?"

"Nothing, I think . . ."

He smiled as only the most highly evolved monsters know how to smile. I was already trembling, because this time he would be the one to pull me along with him among secret things.

Three days have passed since that afternoon, and still I haven't been able to shake off the spell cast by what I saw. But more than anything, I now know that wanting to help Felice was an act of presumption that the gods have punished by flinging me down into an abyss where everything is possible, and everything reversible.

After he moved the pieces of that giant king-size bed which I had never seen assembled, there appeared in the wall a small door, one that looked made for a dwarf. It was locked—but Felice had the key! The fact that he had never mentioned it in all those years was already peculiar; but that in the midst of his disintegrating memory he had been able to find that key—a key presumably unused since the day my grandfather had bought the property—was even more astonishing. And from the way he opened the little door, I understood that even if my amnesiac could on any given day forget his own name or the word for lettuce, he knew exactly what we would find in there.

He knew it with such certainty that, in the darkness stinking of mildew and saltpeter, he immediately pointed the flashlight at the precise spots where it needed to be pointed, without any useless fluttering. And those three spots corresponded to the greatest thing a young boy could ever see: three skeletons! Better yet, three skeletons in SS uniforms—uniforms that, despite their tears and holes, had kept the bones interconnected in the final poses of the deceased. I would have stayed there looking at them for hours, bewitched, if Felice hadn't grabbed me by my arm and pulled me away.

"Was us tha' killt 'em," he said, putting back the pieces of the bed.

Not just a monster, but a hero too!

"You who?"

"Me, Giuàn, an' Carmen."

Carmen—I knew her! A tranquil woman, always tending to her house and garden, who never failed to smile at me when I passed her on my bicycle.

And so he told me the story. He told me that when the German army was retreating, those three—an officer and two soldiers—arrived in Nasca after having separated from the rest; that they plundered one house after the other, roughing people up as they went, and that when Piero, the town idiot, didn't understand what they wanted from him, they shot two bullets into his head and left him lying in the middle of the road in a pool of his own blood; that after this, Giovanni had called him and Carmen to set a trap, and the three Germans took the bait like suckers, that the word "prosciutto" was enough to lure them into that little room, where they were then beaten with sickles and awls, and left locked up to bleed to death, an outcome that was verified the next day, the date that tiny door was opened for the last time.

"And the Kropoffs, where were they when all this was happening?"

"Dunno, down in the cellar pissin' 'emselves, hidin' in the woods . . . Dunno."

"And they never found out a thing?"

"Nothin' at all—not the Kropoffs an' not yer gran'parents neither."

"And Giovanni?"

"Dead an' gone, Giuàn is."

"And Carmen?"

"Carmen don' say a word."

"You killed one of them yourself?"

"One each, so."

"And how did you ..."

"The sickle, a clout to the gull't till he were stone dead!"

"Well done! I'm literally in awe."

"Sure 'twere well done, blast it! Not tha' I done it for me country—done it for Piero."

"I would have too."

"Oh shush, y'are jus' a wee lad!"

"And you can't remember if your father was alive or dead when this happened? Whether he was or wasn't around? You don't remember at all?"

He shook his head like a hippopotamus trying to shake water out of its ears.

"And why, after so long, have you shared this secret with me now?"

"'Cause maybe migh' help for fin'in' me da."

"Three Nazi corpses? I doubt it. If I asked you to picture your dad in uniform, could you?"

"Course!"

"And what's the uniform like?"

"Beaut'ful, chrisomighty's it beaut'ful! Firs', two boots, but the tall kin', up o'er the knees, like ... then white trousers, tight like yer lasses' tights ... an' a blue coat, but long, ye see? Long on the sides an' behint, wi' two wha' ye call 'em like brushes on the sho'ders ... then a white shirt, all 'mbroidered ... an' then ...

an' then a funny-lookin' hat, like 'em Russians wear, black an' long . . . an' the sword! A curved an' shiny one—blazes, 'ow beaut'ful . . ."

He was describing a hussar or a dragoon, or an officer of Napoleon's Old Guard . . . But where did that image come from? Only one thing was certain: in that moment, he was *seeing* him.

"Tell me something: have you actually seen your dad dressed like that, or did you just give me this answer because I asked you to imagine your father in uniform?"

"A'tually seen 'im so."

"Many times?"

"On'y way t' be seein' 'im!"

"And you're telling me this *now*?"

"Asked me afore an' I'd a' tol' ye."

"Unbelievable! So you don't remember his face, but you do remember his uniform!"

He nodded as though completely indifferent to the points I was making.

"This wouldn't happen to be like Aurelio Fierro all over again, would it?"

"Wha' d'ye mean?"

"I mean that maybe one day you saw a nineteenth-century officer in a Liebig card, and for some reason you associate that image with your father. Like with Cellini's salamander, it's always the same story."

For a second, I wondered whether I should talk to him about Pavlov, but having read only a few scattered things on the subject I didn't feel sufficiently equipped to give him a lesson on conditioned reflexes. Sure, *Pavlov's Ships* was one of the best Urania sci-fi books to come out in recent memory, but still . . . I wondered if what he said about actively keeping that secret hidden since 1945 was also false, in the sense that the episode had actually faded into oblivion many years ago, and he had only now recalled it. Or maybe it was a true case of paramnesia, with Felice having only witnessed actions carried out by others. Regardless, that room was a real secret room, and he was the one with the key. What disconcerted me the most, however, was the seamless continuity between the Germans and the hussar. For memories were not only ephemeral in my patient's mind, but transitive. Pushkin, Foscolo, Napoleon, the French retreat from Russia, the Germans, Neapolitan songs, slugs, lettuce—everything stuck to and implicated the rest.

I asked my grandfather if any objects in the house had once belonged to the Kropoffs. After several requests for clarification, I gathered that they couldn't correspond to more than a fifth of the house's total contents, seeing as the rest—just as old, if not older—was the fruit of my grandfather's antiquarian passions: the majority of the prints, the pewter, the art books, the crystal glasses, the silverware, the ivory and jade, the rugs and the chinoiserie, all of it had to be excluded from the reconstructed inventory. Of the objects left over from the Russians, many had to be similarly excluded, because their weight and bulk would have rendered their transportation from the motherland impossible, especially during an emergency; and others, even if less cumbersome, had no doubt already been in the house at the time of their arrival, since they reflected the typical craftsmanship of the area. It's true that my monster, if he had really grown up in that house, wouldn't be able to distinguish between preexisting items and items brought from Russia, but I firmly believed in the energy that certain things can absorb and later unleash in unexpected forms; and, intuiting that when people leave their homeland in a hurry, with no hope of ever returning, they try to take with them their most cherished objects, the ones that are most imbued with sentimental value or most representative of what they are about to lose, I was confident that if I could pinpoint one of those objects, he and I would obtain from it a sort of illumination. That year at school, we had read about Aeneas's flight from burning Troy, and I had learned that the Lares stay tied to a place, whereas the Penates go with the family. All I needed to do was get my hands on the Penates of the Kropoffs.

The Penates of the Kropoffs . . . The most precious of these, of course, must have followed them on their subsequent move too; but more than once my grandfather had stressed how they'd left in a hurry, taking next to nothing with them. And so there was hope that something meaningful had been left behind. But what? Various objects were still on display in the living and dining rooms, but what did this privilege signify, if not that the new owner's tastes had vampirically reincorporated them, as the ancient Romans did with the statues of their conquered peoples' divinities? It was likely that the energy introduced into them by my grandfather had, if not substituted, then at the very least contaminated their original aura; or else those objects, left to languish in such a degraded state, had little by little lost the power once vested in them . . .

I therefore chose not to probe that browned silver pill case, nor that little St. Cyril icon, nor that alabaster ampoule—a luxury I could afford because, almost right after moving in, my grandfather had taken the majority of that Kropoffian heritage and thrown it into the fruit room. And if something still pulsed with energy, it was there, among those relics, that it lay hidden.

The fruit room, located on the top floor, was thus called because it was full of shelves on which, in accordance with the season, apples were stored and walnuts were left to dry, persimmons to ripen, grapes to shrivel up into raisins; and even when empty, the room retained a sweetish, moldy smell that made your head spin, and in all these years I've never understood whether it was the nicest and most tantalizing smell in the world or the most disgusting.

The shelves toward the back of the room, meanwhile, had always been used to store the most disparate things: spare tiles, two old Flobert air rifles, empty bottles, old toys, and a considerable number of boxes. At least two of these boxes, my grandfather had told me, contained the Kropoffs' belongings. So as not to disorient my memoryless friend, I decided to make a preliminary selection; then, equipped with a dozen objects, I led him behind the sweet Osmanthus while my grandparents were sleeping. I took a good look at him: from up close, his skin looked macerated, the smallpox scars appearing less clearly defined but wider; and even the veins covering his nose seemed to radiate outward, as if their color had bled into the surrounding skin. His old winish birthmark now looked as though it, too, had expanded, and I don't know if it was merely a trick of the imagination, but I could have sworn that on the back of his right hand another splotch of sediment was forming. His eyelids, glued down more by muscular tension than by his resinous pinkeye, gave no hint as to where he was looking. Probably, I was merely crouching next to a poor soul suffering from senile dementia, but something, something that I refused to attribute to all the tales of American Indians I had seen at the movies, persuaded me I was conversing with a wise man or soothsayer.

The first object I handed him was a lacquered box full of buttons—with those eyelids of his, there was almost no need to tell him to keep his eyes closed. He held the box in his hands, then shook it, the buttons rustling like gravel in a creek.

"So? Do you see anything?"

"I see . . . see . . ."

"Yes?"

"See feck all!"

My impatience was rattling him. I silently handed him a fan. Apparently recognizing what the object was, he wasted no time in opening it, but the fabric immediately ripped in multiple spots. Disgusted, he threw it aside without a word. I picked a craquelé vase, the kind with a thin neck, for a single rose. This time he paid closer attention, caressing the object for a while in order to understand its function.

"Mm, like this—shaped like a pear, so."

I kept quiet.

"Pears . . . oh, pear trees's darlin' things, I used say so t' 'im, to the boss, but he weren't wantin' 'em."

"Who did you used to say it to, to Mr. Kropoff?"

"T' yer granda, I used say it."

"But my grandfather still has you planting pear trees!"

"The one now, ay. But th' other, not at all."

"Which other one?"

"Th' other, the one tha's dead."

"Do you mean Mr. Kropoff brought his father here too?"

"Ach, g'wan."

"Well then, what are you talking about?"

"Abou' yer granda, but the dead one."

A shudder ran through me, because words such as these can create any sort of truth.

"And when did he die, this other grandfather?"

"Eh . . . when I were jus' a lad, chrissake."

"And he was named Giuseppe too?"

"Giusepp', think so."

"And my grandmother?"

"No, she weren't 'ere. Sure y'are not always needin' women roun' ye!"

"But if the Russians were here, how could my grandfather have been here too?"

"Maybe 'imself were also a Russian."

"And where does your dad come in to all this?"

"Me da be the key t' it all: fin' 'im, an' we're grand."

"Ah, because everything else seems logical to you."

"Oui, mon jeune ami, très logique."

"What did you say?!"

"When?"

"Just now: 'Oui, mon jeune ami . . .'"

"I says me da be the key 's all."

"No, after that."

"Nothin'."

"No, you spoke in French. Do you realize what just happened? You're holding a Russian vase and you spoke in French, the way upper-class Russians did before the revolution."

"Rev'lution?"

"The Communist revolution! You must have seen the movies with Don Camillo and Peppone!"

"Michelín."

"What?"

"Feelin' knackered, can't be takin' no more o' this carry-on . . . Can't I jus' be havin' no mem'ry an' bugger the res'?"

"Of course you can, if that's what you want. But it's not a pretty thing, to wake up in the morning and not even remember your name."

"An' righ' y'are, but 'nough now. Time to be goin' home an' goin' asleep."

He stood up slowly as if disentangling himself from the earth, handed me the vase, and walked off looking more hunched than usual. After a few steps, however, he stopped, and without turning around said, "So ye says I were talkin' like 'em slugs?"

"Even if red slugs are French, they don't speak the French language! You spoke like the French, like French people!"

"An' me da, 'ow the divil'd he talk?"

"I don't know. Either Italian, or Russian, or French. Or a dialect."

"An' the bes'?"

"Depends. No language is the absolute best."

"But the dead, the dead likes Frensh . . ."

He had a way of surprising you, suddenly opening frightening windows onto things that he couldn't possibly know . . . or could he? And I had the weakness of always letting myself be carried away by him, rather than steering the conversation.

"The dead? And when have you heard the dead talking?"

"Always."

"But do you see them too? Where are they?"

"Righ' 'ere, undergroun'. They're all roun', so: in the sod under th' orchard, under the larch, behin' the nettles, by the haylof', under 'em pear trees, 'em ches'nut trees, 'em medlars an' arbors . . ."

"And what about in the rest of the town? Farther out in the countryside?"

He shook his head. "Jus' 'ere."

"What do you mean 'just here'? A whole graveyard of Frenchmen, right under our feet—only here, on our property?"

"Ay."

"And since when have you heard them talking?"

"Since I were a young fella."

"And it never scared you?"

"Sure the dead be dead, can't do nothin' no more."

"But how can you say for sure that they speak French if you don't know the language?"

"If they're Frensh, they wants t' be talkin' Frensh."

"But this is a vicious cycle! How can you know that they're French?"

"For they're the ones is sen'in' up the slugs."

There it was, the key to his obsessions—his father was minor in comparison: those cursed red slugs which I was nearly beginning to hate myself.

"An' thinkin' 'f it now, th' other granda, from afore, he was eaten up 'live by 'em slugs, an' so 'twere he come to be dead."

"Did you see this happen yourself?"

"Giuàn seen it."

"Speaking of which, the three Germans never talk?"

"Have t' be undergroun' to talk, all the way down. 'Nough now, goin' home."

He walked off, swaying as if from immense exhaustion. He was the earthiest, the most torpid being I knew, and yet something mesmeric dwelled in him, like an inner beam of light bouncing all around in search of a way out. And while I felt disheartened by the impossibility of helping him to put his unsettled mind back in order, there now crept in the joy of being able to confirm that my monster truly was a monster.

So, my mnemonic assistance was proving to be a failure. It's true that it had remedied a few urgent issues, but at what cost? At the cost of both of us entering a dimension where logic, experience, chronology, and the laws of physics had lost all value. Was it really worth teaching him how to recall the taste of a sausage or the name of a vegetable, if in so doing we found ourselves surrounded by Russians, by Frenchmen, by the dead, by mischievous and malevolent spirits who had fun at our expense with their linguistic babel? Nor could a fact both consoling and humiliating escape me: the true protagonist of these extrasensory experiences was Felice and only Felice, for it was through his mouth that those demons spoke, he was the one having those visions, he held the golden bough of knowledge and perdition. Me, I was only a secondary figure obliged to play the tedious part of skepticism and common sense; and while I needed to stay clearheaded in order to maintain some hope of success in that undertaking, my whole being was instead dying to cohere with that world of illusions, a world where a company of Napoleonic soldiers had trained an underground army of red slugs to rise up to the surface and devour my *first* grandfather! What an amazing story! And yet I had to say no and resist the sirens, at least until Felice solved the mystery of his father, a mystery that tortured him so, and around which everything revolved as in a whirlpool.

I let a few days pass, then once again subjected him to an examination of the Russian objects. One after the other, they passed through his bloated and cut-up hands without arousing the slightest reaction. Except the last in the series, an antique pen made of wood with a brass nib ring; the nib itself was missing, however, and when I shook the pen, some dust that had once been ink came out. Rubbing that dust between my fingertips, I saw that it must have been purple ink, a favorite among nineteenth-century ladies. I placed his hand around the pen as though he needed to write. It was like switching on a radio.

"Mon aimé et malheureux fils . . ."

I kept silent for a moment longer, but he had frozen.

"And then?"

"Mon aimé et malheureux fils . . . fils . . ."

"Who's writing, a man or a woman?"

"Yerself, Michelín."

"Me?"

"Insi' o' me . . . ye yerself 'tis."

So, now it was no less than a matter of telepathy. I had built myself a little nineteenth-century novel full of anagnorises and dramatic twists, and I *wanted* Felice to embody and to give voice to that novel, deriving it from the energy unleashed by that pen, which instead released nothing but a puff of purple dust. If this was the case, then I was the most disruptive and confusing element of all—I who therefore needed to find a way not to interfere so violently.

"Wha' language were it, Frensh?"

"Yes, French."

"Michelín."

"Still here."

"Ye ain't dead, like?"

"Why? Now French is only the language of the dead?"

"The Frensh ought t' all be stayin' undergroun', tha' be the righ' place for 'em."

"You do know, though, that they fought against the Germans in the war?"

"An' so?"

"If you killed Germans, you were on the side of the French."

"Are ye mad? Meself, wi' 'em Frensh?"

"But not with the Germans either."

"Wi' no one, blast it!"

"And what if the French buried beneath us were killed by the Germans?"

"'En I says: fair play, Germans!"

"And the Russians?"

"Russians can go buggerin' off ta hell."

"Well then, all accounted for."

"Michelín."

"Yes?"

"Now I tell ye somethin', but I tell ye on'y once: Lake Maggior', it does be havin' its laws, y'understan'? Its own laws."

Incredible . . . not even Lovecraft gave me such chills when he wrote of the Mountains of Madness . . . The laws of Lake Maggiore! What need was there to force my Pushkinesque novel on Felice, when he himself dazzled me with lines such as this? Lake Maggior', it does be havin' its laws: a sentence like that was alone enough to make existence ten times more interesting.

But what did the laws of Lake Maggiore mean? That here, being Russian, French, or German was no longer all that important; in fact, it probably didn't matter at all. But being dead or alive didn't make much of a difference either, if there were two versions of my grandfather roaming about, the same exact grandfather, though one living and one dead . . . Yet despite such corrosive laws, Felice's father remained important. Why? Because he had passed down the hereditary curse of amnesia? Or—but could it be?—were the slugs really what turned him into a figure of consequence? Among my books was a copy of Sigmund Freud's *The Interpretation of Dreams*, and I remembered that in that thin yellow volume the image of the slug was described on several occasions as charged with sexual meanings, which all happened to be utterly theoretical and abstract for me: once, it was the female genitalia, then a male organ in terribly bad shape, then it was cited for the allusive nature of its hornlike tentacles. But could an image that symbolized such disparate things really symbolize anything? Moreover, those meanings concerned dreams, and far too many times I had run up against the impossibility of wringing even the vaguest snippet of a dream from Felice. And besides, what need did a man like that have to dream anyway—one who hears voices chattering in French under heads of lettuce?

The secret little room with the German bodies . . . the back of the fruit room . . . Who could say if our house had other places such as these . . . maybe even a trapdoor or a hidden passageway known only to the Kropoffs, or to whomever had built the place . . . Of course, Felice's small and solitary living quarters couldn't offer much in that regard, which suggested once again that what we were searching for was, instead, close to me . . . But a house is like a mind, with its enigmas and its obscure circumvolutions, its ambiguities and its obsessions . . . When roaming through the rooms and hallways, going up and down from one floor to the next, I truly had the impression that I was moving inside my own head, and not only because there wasn't a single mildew stain or air bubble imprisoned in glass that did not speak to me of myself, of the inestimable degree of melancholy or anguish or boredom that had accompanied my seeing it; but also because the very structure of the house had by now been so thoroughly internalized as to have spread to my mind, reshaping it.

In this building lived monsters, my monsters. I had always known it, and had therefore always done everything in my power to befriend them. Some inspired tenderness, some terrified me, but for all of them I harbored an immense respect, growing sincerely fond of them over time—because I had no others to keep me company, in life. Compared to them, Felice was a pseudo-monster: compared, I mean, to the Monster in the Woodshed or to the Larva or to that nameless entity who stared at the nape of my neck but whom I was never fast enough to see when I abruptly turned around. Yes, he was considerably ugly, he had a face bloated and deformed by growths, cavities, marks, scars; he had that purple . . . those encrusted and perennially shut eyes . . . he hawked phenomenal gobs of spit . . . then there was his intimacy with the terrible verdigris, as though immune to the poison, and the violence with which he butchered and skinned rabbits . . . But was all this sufficient to turn him into a monster, or had my own will to supplement these qualities been necessary from the beginning? His recent memory loss, meanwhile—didn't it only help to humanize him? And yet . . . and yet his mental unraveling was granting him a visionary power which, if falling short of making him a monster, did put him in contact with something frightening and unhuman . . . with the dead, essentially, although at this point I honestly needed to establish on a theoretical level what the relationship was between dead people and monsters, between mortality and monstrosities . . . For example, it would have been difficult to assert that the dead were unhuman . . . And herein lay the other thorny question: whether it was permissible or even imperative to distinguish between silent dead and talking dead, between absent dead and present dead . . . But I was thirteen and a half: could I set out to answer such gravely momentous questions? Better for me simply to stick to wishing the Larva goodnight every evening before bed, and to trying to slow, by any available means, Felice's descent into the abyss of amnesia.

And Felice himself—this is the point I wanted to make—by now lived permanently among the house's mysteries and, therefore, inside of me. He slept in his little room, worked in our garden and orchard, but it was in my head that he searched for his father.

The more I racked my brains, the clearer it became that the biggest aporia in the whole story was the mother's absence, the son's total lack of interest. I was reluctant to discard it, but clearly the tale of the maidservant's son unacknowledged by the younger Kropoff didn't hold water. At the same time, if Felice had been abandoned as a baby, on the doorstep of some convent, why in the world would the Kropoffs have been the ones to take him in? Maybe the mother died while bringing him into the world, and young Kropoff, out of love for the deceased, had taken in the newborn, putting him in the care of one of their maidservants; but then why not officially recognize the child? Maybe because the mother was a commoner? Because old Kropoff had vetoed it? And when the child was old enough to understand, what was he told about his mother? Whether true or false, at the very least he should have remembered it—but no, nothing. I spoke with Carmen, too, naturally without saying a word about the three Germans; but she, like everyone else, couldn't recall Felice as ever being anything other than a solitary man whose familial ties were a complete mystery. It did give me a strange feeling to hear her put into words what I had already found out, namely, that he had worked on our property his whole life, first for the Kropoffs, then for my grandfather.

It wasn't until that night, twisting and turning in my overgrown cast-iron bed, that I did the math: the year being 1969, if Felice was somewhere between fifty-eight and sixty then he must have been born between 1909 and 1911. But the Kropoffs couldn't have arrived any earlier than 1917: actually, it was a well-known fact that, before finding a place to settle permanently, Russians fleeing the revolution often stayed in Switzerland for a period of time, making 1918 the most likely year of their arrival.

So in Felice's life there had been a pre-Kropoffian phase that corresponded to his childhood, during which, I hoped, he hadn't already started to work in the house as a child slave.

I addressed the matter with him the next day.

"Afore 'em Russians?"

"Yes, when you were very little."

"I were there." And with an imprecise wave, he gestured toward the shed where the rabbits were kept.

"What do you mean 'there'? What was there back then?"

"'Twere the same: rabbiss."

"You mean that you lived with the rabbits?"

"Ay."

"Do you realize what you're saying?"

He hawked loudly. "A cancer strike me if t'ain't so."

"But there must have been someone who took care of you, right?"

"Ay, th' Great Rabbit."

If I hadn't been certain that he didn't know who Lewis Carroll was, I would have sworn he was pulling my leg. I tried not to lose my patience.

"Tell me about this Great Rabbit."

"He were beaut'ful, blast me if he weren't beaut'ful . . . an' he were the bigges' of 'em all, the like to be weighin' a hundr'd poun's, till ye'd be callin' 'im a great big rabbit . . . Shame he hadn't no eyes on 'im . . ."

A hundred-pound rabbit with no eyes . . . Before I could even decide how to take this story I was already completely enchanted by it. I was the child, and he the nursemaid.

"And why didn't he have eyes?"

"The Frensh ript 'em ou' wi' a wee spoon . . . Ye see, those Frensh bastar's? Was 'imself taught me t' be cuttin' the slugs in two, wi' his big buck teet' . . ."

Oh yes, those French were beginning to go too far, and their slugs no longer seemed all that defensible to me . . .

"And until what point did you live with the rabbits?"

"Long as th' Great Rabbit were still 'live."

"And how old were you?"

"I . . . dunno . . . nine, ten—sure who knows . . ."

"And that's when the Kropoffs found you?"

"Dunno, dunno . . . don't 'member nothin' . . . it be all dark, like . . . dark an' black . . . We'd be needin' the eyes o' th' Great Rabbit for t' see somethin' . . . I know where the Frensh hid 'em, but none can be goin' there, no."

So the eyes of this enormous rabbit were hidden somewhere in the garden or in the woodshed or in the hayloft, or even in our house . . . and the truth was still stamped in those retinas—in them the story of Felice's father was told. But what terrible taboo forbade him from retrieving them? I couldn't glean any hints, because he clamped his eyelids even more tightly shut, and even pressed his lips together the way children do to send the message that they'll be keeping as silent as the grave; and all the while he stayed crouched down in the grass next to me, lightly swaying forward and back like an old medicine man mentally reciting his prayers. Far, far away—in that moment, he was worlds away from me, and never, since the beginning of that whole story, had I felt so lost in a senseless universe. After a long and painful silence, during which I, too, had started to sway, I cast all hesitation to the wind and all but assailed him.

"Felice!"

"Wha' ye want?"

"You're convinced that no one can go there, but if you tell me where, I'll go myself."

"Are ye mad?"

"Tell me and I'll go."

"Not on yer life."

"Please . . . I'm not afraid . . . and wouldn't you love to find out something about your father?"

"Michelín."

"At your service."

"Y'ave no idea the dangers . . . ye can't, trus' me, ye can't . . ."

"Nothing will happen to me. I have my good-luck charms."

"Come 'ere t' me, 'em eyes is in the scaries' place in th' 'ole house. I jus' tell ye an' ye be pissin' yer britches wi' fright."

"Tell me."

"No."

"Tell me."

"The cellar."

"Great, I'll go to the cellar."

"To the cellar me arse, blast'd son 'f a dog!"

"You can't stop me. It's my house."

Here he laughed with amusement, without a hint of sarcasm or provocation: pure amusement.

"Yers! Ha! 'His' says he, tha' house there! Sure 'tis meself pissin' his britches now, but for laughin'!"

"Why? Whose house is it, then?"

"'Em down b'low."

"The French?"

"B'low I says, not undergroun'."

"And what does down below mean?"

"Down b'low means in the cellar! D'ye still not understan' it be down there tha' all things is d'cided?"

"That's exactly why I want to go there."

"Think caref'lly abou' it, Michelín, 'cause were there yer grandas was swished."

A masterful teller of tales: the switching of the grandfathers . . . The spirit of writers like Hoffmann, Poe, and Lovecraft lived again in him, the verdigris man . . .

"Let me point out to you that, for strictly chronological reasons, my real grandfather is the current one and only the current one."

"Ah get 'way outa tha'! This one now be a copy, the real one were the firs'."

"But it's not possible! My grandfather bought this house in 1955, the year I was born! Before then he never set foot on the property."

"Michelín."

"Wha' now!"

"Y'ever asked yerself why yer granda knows nothin' abou' meself?"

I didn't answer, gripped simultaneously by distress and euphoria.

"'Cause he knowed me when I were a'ready big an' grown, an' he ne'er asked me a thing . . . But th' other granda, he seen me grow, seen me as a lad, he knowed me da . . ."

"Well then, is my mother the daughter of the first one or the second? Whose grandson am I?"

"Ah, if ye don' know 't yerself . . ."

"Listen, we started all of this to help fix your memory, mine is fine as it is."

"S'long as y'are happy . . ."

"Happy, no—but at least I know how things have gone in my life."

"This be wha' ye b'lieve . . . wha' they makes ye b'lieve."

"They who?"

"'Em in the cellar."

"But if what you say is true, why for all these years did you never warn me when you knew I was going down to the cellar?"

"'Cause ye was goin' to play, not searsh."

"But how do you know? Often, in fact, the game I was playing was none other than searching."

"Ay, but ye didn't know wha' t' be searshin' for."

"And they could tell the difference, if I went down with the aim of finding the rabbit's eyes?"

"Ah, if tha's wha' y'are aimin' for, ye be lookin' a long time . . ."

"Is that so?"

"When we're gabbin', they're lis'nin' t' ev'ry word . . ."

"Felice, you know what I think? That these beings exist only in your head."

"Ah, could be, for is 'emselves eatin' me mem'ries . . ."

"Even the location of your toilet, they ate that too?"

"Tha' too. Sure when it comes to doin' mishief on a fella . . ."

"But why would they be so thoroughly out to get you?"

"For me da: went eatin' his thoughts too."

"But what do you mean by 'eat them'? Erase them?"

"No, no, eat, I says, an' d'ye know 'ow they do be eatin' 'em?"

I didn't speak, too busy trying to hold back my brain from jumping ahead and imagining the answers.

"By turnin' inta slugs! An' once insi', say g'bye to yer thoughts, 'cause 'em slugs is eatin' 'em up in no time at all."

Horror! A brain swarming with slugs sucking on its synapses! Suddenly I had a vision of Felice's father shooting himself in the head to escape that torture. For now, his son merely exterminated the slugs in the garden, but maybe the day would come when he'd follow in his father's footsteps.

Not knowing what to say, I asked the first thing that popped into my head.

"Felice, why is verdigris only used for the grapes?"

"Made for grapes, sure."

"But if it kills the parasites on the grapes, it could also be used for other fruits and vegetables . . ."

"Dunno, jus' know 'twere always so."

"And if we tried to use it on other vegetables? Lettuce, for instance?"

"Lettuce?"

"Don't you think that you could put an end to your war with the slugs that way? They'd arrive, eat the verdigris, and die. And maybe, if there are a few around when you spray it, they'll turn turquoise all over. No more red slugs: just turquoise or dead ones."

He stayed quiet and still, clearly tempted. The aspect that probably appealed to him most was the idea of coating with verdigris those foul, chomping creatures. And sure enough:

"Ev'n the slime'd be turnin' turcuss?"

"Even the slime, I think."

"But then we'd have to give tha' lettuce o' yers a fierce wash, like. I dunno 'f yer granda'd be approvin'."

"I'll convince my grandfather, you just worry about the verdigris."

"Ay, but the point?"

"It's a warning to the ones in the cellar, don't you see? You say that they listen to our conversations? Well then, listen up, all of you down there: leave my friend alone, otherwise we'll come down with two tanks and spray verdigris everywhere!"

"Sure y'are ravin' now!"

"It's the only way: make a counterattack. Didn't you say you saw your father with boots and a saber, like a military officer? If he were here, he'd say the same thing." I should have felt guilty exploiting his father like that, but I was evidently the first person to be convinced by the things I made up.

"Tha'd be why they killt 'im."

"Then admit that you're afraid."

"Blazes 'm I afeard, afeard o' the divil, like!"

"Yet you want to find your father."

"I . . . I were wantin' to fin' the face on 'im, his name, to 'member me an' 'im together—tha's what I wanted to fin', not 'imself now!"

Finally, the misunderstanding had been laid bare. In his inability to distinguish the name from the thing, the sign from the signified, Felice had taken my latest moves and suggestions as attempts to arrive not at the faded idea of his father, but—dead or alive (not an altogether decisive distinction for him)—at the *actual person* of his father . . . Mentally backtracking over our recent conversations, I realized that my words really had lent themselves to that interpretation, which prompted a retrospective yet voluptuous shudder . . . But I also knew that if his father was dead, I was not the least bit interested in meeting him, and if he was alive, I was even less so, for what could be enchanting about a ninety-year-old Russian exile who had been living on the French Riviera for the last forty years? And, above all, what would father and son have to say to each other now? Why become responsible for such a miserable encounter? The father would be ashamed of his son and of his own behavior all those years ago, while the son wouldn't recognize the father and would only be left confused—so why bother? Better if he were dead and buried, and better not to know where he was buried . . . In an anthology of dark tales, I had read a story by Jean Paul, who wrote that in every field where a particularly bloody battle had been fought, the dead soldiers convened each year on the battle's anniversary, talking and fraternizing with one another the whole night long . . . But the story seemed to have been referring to ghosts, not corpses buried underground. Additionally, Felice only heard French, whereas according to Jean Paul's theory, he should have heard at least two languages, and only once a year . . .

I decided to forget about the French for now and return to the rabbits. I asked if he didn't feel guilty whenever he killed one of his old childhood companions.

"Not like they're the same or nothin' . . ."

"They're still rabbits, though. What would the Great Rabbit say?"

"Lis'n 'ere, the less ye be talkin' abou' th' Great Rabbit, the be'er."

"Did Carmen ever meet this rabbit?"

"Carmen killt Germans, not rabbiss."

"That's not an answer."

"Giuàn knowed 'im."

"I bet he did . . ."

"An' why?"

"Because he's dead and can no longer say a thing."

"Sure y'are still but a wee lad t' be sayin' the like." After these words, he walked off toward the gate. When I caught up to him, he was already on the road.

"What's that supposed to mean?"

"'Cause if ye don' understan' the dead've more talk in 'em than the livin', y'are yet t' understan' a thing."

He went through the front door, disappearing into his house. I was left feeling so upset that I decided in that instant to go down into the cellar.

The cellar held no secrets for me. A narrow and slippery stairway led, right beyond a small vestibule containing a wall-to-wall cupboard missing its doors, to a large vaulted space cluttered with old vats and barrels, not to mention bottles and miscellaneous crockery. Other bottles rested on the shelves of two tall and narrow recesses that sank into the walls. The only feeble source of light was a grate facing the backyard, located exactly at ground level. The gloomy half-light, the vaulted ceiling, the partially busted barrels, the ancient spiderwebs forming veritable curtains, and finally, the numerous and variously shaped hooks and chains hanging from the ceiling, turned that cellar into a perfect Piranesian etching; and I—obviously I relished being down there, and the more I told myself terrifying stories, the more I relished it. Once, when I was alone in the house and it was already autumn, I waited for dusk before going down into the cellar, completely naked, with a burning candle in hand: if ever anyone had willingly dived into the role of sacrificial offering, it was me.

In there, I had spent an incalculable amount of time over the years: adjusting my eyesight to the faint glow from the grate, I'd examine the labels on the bottles, some of which were so old and so unusually shaped as to surely predate my grandfather's purchase of the house; others, with now illegible handwritten labels, contained a dense and compact substance, which I'd been told had once been must. Felice himself confirmed that the Kropoffs had tried to make wine, but his and their own ignorance of the process had produced disastrous results. Those bottles, in fact, were merely the proof of a final, abandoned attempt. As for my grandfather, he never wanted to hear so much as a word about winemaking, but being a glutton for grapes, he had let the usage of verdigris continue unchanged.

So, there I was in my cellar: could I really be afraid? In that place, I had conversed with every kind of imaginary monster— it would take more than the warnings of my semi-monster to scare me. Somewhere down there, he had said, were hidden the Great Rabbit's eyes, and somewhere, or rather everywhere, were the entities that didn't want to let me find them. In any event, breaking with routine, I'd brought with me a battery-powered flashlight, and with it I started to illuminate the shelves in the two recesses. Old bottles of Crodino, of lemon soda, of Marie Brizard . . . an old Punt e Mes . . . a jar of Citrosodina and one of Citroepatina, the kind I used to steal from my grandparents to make fizzy lemonade . . . all items I knew by heart . . . until, in the corner of the highest shelf in the second recess, I spotted a more muted reflection, seemingly not from glass though nevertheless from something shiny . . . shiny and slimy . . . I slid the flashlight farther inside to better illuminate the object. Yes, it truly was slimy, but it wasn't an eye . . . it was a slug! A red slug, paralyzed with fear! A slug in the cellar, in the dust, on a slate shelf? 'Em slugs! I heard Felice's voice, his terror. I redirected the light at the bottles and demijohns on the floor, examining them one by one: on the neck of one bottle, another slug was slowly climbing toward the top, leaving a wet trail on the dusty exterior, while a third slug had fallen inside a demijohn and was embroidering the glass bottom, uselessly crisscrossing over its own tracks. I looked at it with an impassivity intended to show any hypothetical observers how much I scorned danger, but I was beginning to get a bad feeling. Then I had to inflict the worst on myself.

The vats and the barrels, as I mentioned, were almost all busted and rotten: only one was left with staves still held together with metal hoops—uncoincidentally the smallest one. In those casks, on which, a couple of years earlier, I had stuck a label that read "Amontillado," I imagined lurked every kind of horror: sometimes it was the Gurgler, other times it was an enormous worm coiled around itself, others still it was the tunnel that would suck you down into the Other World . . . It was therefore with a false lightheartedness that I pushed off the lid of that barrel and pointed my flashlight. Horror! Horror both physical and metaphysical! Glimmering in the beam of light, in that barrel there swarmed thousands and thousands of red slugs—and never, I say never, had I seen slugs move so quickly, so that they were more like darting fish trapped in a net . . . I continued to stare, petrified: some of those slugs were noticeably bigger than usual, big enough to resemble sea cucumbers, though all of them, the big as well as the small, fought to remain on the surface, continually replacing one another in a reshuffling that pushed upward from the bottom and downward from the top . . . and the entirety of that thing sounded as though it were *gurgling*—yes, there it was, the Gurgler I had imagined for years, only now it wasn't a charming monster, now it was merely a nauseating foulness that could not even be adorned with a fairy-tale name. Now there were only the damned red slugs, Frensh slugs . . .

It had always been my way never to harm any animals, including the ones most persecuted by others. I was a friend and protector of spiders, of ants, of centipedes, of our local and innocuous little scorpions, of dragonflies, of lizards and geckos, of beetles and earwigs and slugs . . . But now something had changed, now I understood that Felice's haunting fixation was not completely unfounded . . . Whether French or not, those slugs weren't normal, they weren't normal and they weren't monsters either, and so they had nothing whatsoever to justify them . . . I observed the horrid gully in which they wallowed by the thousands, each one soaking itself in the other's slime, a slime that, when added to the rest, did not dry into an iridescent lacquer but produced a foamy glue, a vile thing that had something to do with the word *secretion*, and therefore with an even viler secret . . . But that secretion was not secretive, it was scandalously exuberant, like the foam left over from must which should have rightfully encrusted those barrels . . . And why were they all in there together? Were they mating with one another? Licking one another? Mutually transmitting their terrible knowledge? Who had put them in there, and to what end? And what if it was precisely there, underneath that swarming obscenity, that the two eyeballs of the Great Rabbit were hidden? What if it was a personal test? Was I to roll up my sleeve and plunge my arm down? And what if they sucked on my arm like leeches? If they attached themselves to it like suckerfish? Felice had said that those slugs had eaten his father's memories and were now eating his; relative to the possible fate of my arm, how reassuring was this piece of information?

What I proceeded to do was so automatic and mechanical, I feel as if I only performed it in a dream. When in fact I did do it—oh, did I do it. I ran to the woodshed, took an armful of clumps of verdigris without protecting myself, went back down to the cellar, and threw the verdigris into the barrel: immediately, there was a hissing sound, but I didn't want to verify whether it was the actual searing of their flesh or a collective wailing. Lit by the flashlight, the inside of the barrel sparkled with two opposite colors: the red of the slugs and the turquoise of the verdigris, which, upon contact, caused the slugs to writhe and turn brown. In a crazed fit, I grabbed a stick and stirred; I stirred and stirred until, soaked with all that slime, the pieces of verdigris began to dissolve, quickening the slaughter of the gastropods. In the end, what remained was a dark sludge, in which the individual bodies of the tiny beasts could no longer be distinguished from one another: in exchange, one's gaze could now follow the graceful arabesque of turquoise streaks and splotches, which gave the whole a marbled effect.

So, I hadn't taken the eyes, but the entities feared by Felice hadn't taken me either. Walking around the lawn, I wondered why that barrel contained so many slugs. Was it a kind of breeding tank? Impossible, since all of them were already adult slugs, and some were abnormally large. Unless . . . unless the aim was specifically to breed *abnormal* slugs, and the biggest had simply been the fastest to grow . . . But what did they eat? The barrel would've had to be full of lettuce, whereas it only contained slugs . . . Reasoning as Felice, one could suppose that they were being trained to feed off the thoughts and memories of men . . . But most importantly, *who* had put them in there? And what if, instead, no one had poured them in, because there was actually no bottom to that barrel and the slugs had come directly up from underground? What if that barrel was merely the hatchway that opened onto a subterranean sea of *billions* of slugs? If, one fine day, they would swarm out from that opening, to subjugate us all? I continued to channel Felice in my reasoning: if they came up from underground, they had something to do with the French—maybe the French were the ones breeding them, or maybe that relatively new species of red slug was red due to all the French blood that had soaked our land, and that was why Felice considered them French, not because the species had originally come from that country beyond the Alps . . .

What other sources could I turn to at this point? But how stupid of me, I thought, and I ran to the vegetable garden: soon enough, under a head of chicory, I found one, a tiny slug completely covered in dirt. I delicately picked it up and washed it; then I placed it on a dry magnolia leaf and brought it to my grandfather, who, after examining it, admitted to not knowing the name, though he ruled out with absolute certainty the possibility that it was called a "French slug." We went up to the library to consult the zoology manuals: invertebrates, mollusks, gastropods, and finally, the rich world of land snails and slugs. Categorically excluding all the ones with shells, we concentrated on those without, and discovered that three species had flourished in our gardens, all of them belonging to the family Arionidac: the *Arion hortensis*, caramel-colored, up to 5 cm in length; the *Arion empiricorum*, dark brown, up to 10 cm in length; and—there it was!—the *Arion rufus*, reddish brown, up to 15 cm in length! We read and reread, checked multiple books, but nowhere was the slightest reference made to France. For as long as I could remember, I had seen Felice cut them in two with his spade, spit on them, and say contemptuously, "Frensh slug!" Who had planted that idea in his head? His father? Wherever I went looking, I always wound up at the same dead end: his father.

I returned to his house and told him what I had seen and done in the cellar. He laughed, bouncing with every limb, since he didn't believe me in the slightest. I invited him to come down to see for himself, but he refused as though it were a kind of trap. Then he reflected on the stolen verdigris and went into the woodshed, from which he reemerged furious.

"I dunno wha' y'are after doin' wi' me verd'gris, but if ye steal 't again, I'll be givin' ye wha' for."

"What will you do, tell my grandfather?" I replied, with all the arrogance I could muster, just to provoke him.

"Ay, but th' other one."

That shudder, terrible yet wonderful. I wanted more; to me, it seemed that without those fears, life was not worth living.

"And do you know where to find him?"

He nodded with the air of a man possessing profound secrets.

"And where would that be?"

"An' I should be tellin' a blaggar' like yerself!"

"But how do you think I'm supposed to help you if you keep me in the dark about everything you know?"

"Ye was needin' to help me 'member the things I were forgettin', an' no more."

"Yes, but if you first tell me that the slugs eat them, these things, and then that you don't want to know what goes on in the cellar, clearly we can't make much progress . . . What's more, you ought to explain to me how you know all about this first grandfather, who wasn't even yours, while you don't remember anything about your own father . . ."

"'Cause me da, he disappeart, but tha' oul fella, he still be roun' 'ere."

"But wasn't he supposed to be dead?"

"An' so? Dead an' 'ere."

"But has my current grandfather ever noticed that the other's here?"

"Could go lookin' a hundr'd years an' still fin' nothin'."

"So, their lives don't interfere with each other."

"Int'rfere?"

"They don't intersect, they never bother each other . . ."

"Can't at all."

"And why not?"

"Oh 'nough now, blast it, y'are stubb'rn so ye are! Fine, I tell ye why! 'Cause the firs' be insi' the sec'nd—happy?"

"A moment ago you threatened to tell on me to the first one—that means you can decide which of the two grandfathers you want to speak to, is that right?"

"Lookit, when I wants t' be talkin' to yer granda, I says 'Sir Misser.' An' when I wants t' be talkin' to th' other, I jus' star' talkin'."

"That's all?"

He nodded gravely. Forget about monsters: I had before me a creature capable of communicating with different dimensions that were themselves incapable of communicating with one another.

"Tell me this: are there other people like that?"

"'Ow d'ye mean, peoples like tha'?"

"With two . . . two identities, you know, two souls . . . one inside the other."

"Michelín."

"Yes?"

"Wha' d'ye say we star' talkin' abou' somethin' else now, ay?"

Again that shudder, but more agonizing this time—only agonizing, in fact.

"No."

"Michelín."

"Yes."

"Yerself, y'are a person like tha'."

During the following days, I did my best to avoid that man. Before seeing him again, I wanted to get used to the idea that I, too, was a monster. A monster and dead, as far as my first identity was concerned. What he had told me was so overwhelming, I hadn't had the presence of mind to ask him when I had died, at what age, where, if I also had something to do with the Kropoffs, with the French, with his own life story . . . All combinations were possible, and it was enough to let my mind run wild for any solution to find its own fantastic plausibility: the more fantastic, the more plausible. That was what Hoffman wrote, and it was not a coincidence that, even back then, I considered him to be one of the world's greatest writers.

I tried as hard as I could to remember if Felice had two different ways of addressing me, as he did for my grandfather, but only "Michelín" came to mind. "Michelín" or nothing at all, but in both cases the nature of the conversation didn't present any appreciable differences. I thought that perhaps he only wanted to scare me and keep me out of the cellar, but the tone in which he had told me that terrifying thing was a truthful one. Then I thought that he had simply gone mad; actually, I was surprised to realize how long it had taken me to arrive at such a logical conclusion, the only possible conclusion. However, if he had really gone mad, what were all those slugs doing in that barrel? Hercule Poirot would have remarked that when two things inexplicably contradict each other, it means that, in reality, they explain each other, pointing to the conclusion that madness itself had led Felice to fill that barrel with slugs ... Easy to say, but to do? To the naked eye, there couldn't have been fewer than a couple thousand, and how could he have managed to capture and keep alive so many slugs—he who due to an unstoppable urge instinctively cut them in two the moment he saw them? True, he had promised to put an end to that carnage; but could he have procured so many in such a short time? And then there remained the mystery of their nonexistent nourishment ...

Five days after the fact, I returned to the cellar. To convince myself of my own courage, I went in the dark and, halfway down the stairs, even uttered these words: "Oh you who live down here: bugger off ta hell!" Then I turned on the flashlight and illuminated the inside of the barrel. As expected, the little corpses, melded into their slobbery secretions and the dissolved verdigris, had formed a rubbery brownish mass which, when provoked by a stick, still revealed a considerable elasticity, a characteristic that was destined to disappear before long: three days later, upon further inspection, I saw that the blob, at least on its surface, looked glazed or vitrified, a result I attributed entirely to the power of the verdigris.

I took advantage of those two trips to the cellar to look once again for the eyes of the Great Rabbit, even if I was rather skeptical by now. I thought I had found one when I happened to pick up one of those ancient soda bottles. There was a glass marble inside it, and for a moment I wondered if such an object could have been what inspired the story of the eyes in Felice's delirious mind—but this hypothesis seemed so uncharitable that I erased it with an act of surgical volition.

That summer I was thirteen and a half. Now that I am fifty, I can say that nothing has changed since then, because my condition has always been one of doubleness; although I have never succeeded in ascertaining whether this split is only psychological, or ontological too. According to Felice, inside of me lived both a dead person and a living person: must I consider myself a coward if I never wished to get to the bottom of the matter? The charm of that whole story, moreover, was bound up in the fact that it concerned another, not to mention those quintessential *others* who are monsters; but to discover that I, too, was a monster was not so amusing, especially if I had to trust what an old wine-guzzler told me. There, that's how unfair I was: now that I was personally involved, our factotum suddenly became a poor drunkard . . . What's more, it wasn't as though my grandfather, in the wake of Felice's revelations, had gained much in the way of fantastical charm, and neither had I—so what good had come of it all? I wasn't a scientist inquiring out of a love for the truth, I was a fledgling aesthete investigating out of a love for shudders and dramatic effect, and in the absence of similar rewards, I'd go back to the library to live as before . . . But could I explain this to Felice? Could I make him understand that I would be there for him only as long as he guaranteed me an adequate titillation of the nerves and spirit? But this was not completely true either, because I loved that bearish man, and to think of him in his little room searching desperately for objects whose location or name he could no longer remember broke my heart.

Oscillating between these extremes, I began to hate his father as the man responsible for everything. What an arrogant little officer, with his waxed mustache and his contrived quips to impress the ladies . . . What an asshole, in fact, even if he was a hussar or a dragoon—but why ennoble him with that nineteenth-century touch? Couldn't he have been a sleazy dispatch rider for that worm Badoglio? A dirty Fascist of the Muti Legion? As anti-Communist as his son was, he had at least done in a German, which effectively made him a part of the Italian Resistance . . . It was 1969, and I couldn't have known then the meaning of revisionism, couldn't yet appropriately despise those who maintain that Fascism and the Resistance were more or less equivalent . . . Too bad that the pieces didn't fit together because Felice loathed not the Germans, but the French. Why? It was becoming an all-consuming obsession. He hated the French to the point that those slugs had even been Francophied, and he claimed that they conversed in French beneath our land. I wondered if the cause of this could simply have been linguistic transference run amok—say, an insult he received during his childhood from someone named Franco or Francesco—but I was too ignorant on the subject. Or else his father had been a Fascist killed by the French, maybe in Paris, where he had gone to assassinate the Rosselli brothers . . . Good for the French, in that case, but could I tell him that? Besides, deep down I felt that a story of monsters couldn't sink to the level of politics; it had to play out entirely among the natural sciences and the metaphysical, it had to stretch back at the very least to the previous century . . .

I spent a few utterly restless nights, during which every element that had been gained thus far continued to change meaning and significance. Only one thing remained constant: Felice's misogyny. He was male, his father was male, my two grandfathers were male and, whether singular or double, so was I; the Frenchmen were male, the Germans male, Giuàn was male, the Great Rabbit male. In the good as well as the bad, all the principal characters were male, since even the slugs, with their connection to those Frenchmen, appeared to be male in Felice's mind. There was only one exception: Carmen. Felice exhibited the most disconcerting indifference about his mother, he never

named my grandmother nor said a word to her, and even when
he recalled peeling spuds in the kitchen as a child, he was unable
to remember a single female figure around him. Only Carmen
had come up in the things he said: and so I would go once again
to talk to Carmen.

Carmen also lived alone, in a house with a vegetable garden at the end of town. I found her bent over, closely examining her lettuce. Could it be that she, too, was obsessed with slugs?

"Good morning, Mrs. Carmen."

"Ah, it's you."

"Are you checking if there are any slugs?"

"Yes, damned things, there are more than usual this year."

"Which, the red ones?"

"Red, brown, green—they're all slugs."

"So it doesn't make a difference to you?"

"All slugs eat lettuce the same way."

"Oh, so why does Felice have it in for the red ones?"

"You know how he gets things into his head, that man . . ."

"Do I ever . . . You know he talks to me about Frenchmen all the time?"

Was it my frantic desire for the stuff of novels, or did I truly see her grow stiff and her gaze harden?

"Frenchmen? He must be getting confused with the Kropotkins."

"You mean the Kropoff family."

"Kropoff, Kropotkin, either way, they were Russian . . . The ones that lived in your house."

"But how could he confuse Russians and Frenchmen?"

"Why not, seeing as they spoke French?"

"Always?"

"As far as I can remember, always."

Not even in *War and Peace* did characters go so far! The Kropoffs must have been pretty stuck-up to have switched entirely to French. Unless, after the revolution, they considered both Russia and its language to be dead . . . As for the actual members of that family, however, Carmen's memory suddenly began to fade: a man and a woman, maybe a son . . .

"What do you mean, 'maybe'?"

"That, given his age, he could have been just as easily a son as a grandson. And what a fine son, too: he was never around!"

"Never ever?"

"My, how many questions! Never, almost never!"

"But you remember him?"

"Yeah, when he hadn't been here long, but then he disappeared for many years, because when I saw him again he had changed a lot. Then he disappeared again."

"For good?"

"I'm not sure. Once there was a person on the terrace with the old man, but I was too far away to see who it was."

"And what was he like, when he first got here?"

"A tall, good-looking young man, with a mustache."

"And later?"

"Ugly, fat, and no mustache."

"But it was still him?"

"I think so."

She thought so! Even Carmen left a door open to the fantastic . . . I asked her if she knew the reasons for his departure and those rare returns. She shook her head. I asked her the son's name, whereupon she continued to shake her head. I asked if the name Aurelio meant anything to her, and she went on shaking it. I had many more questions to ask, but she was sending the message that, as far as she was concerned, the conversation was over. However, as I left I got the better of her, for once I reached the little gate that enclosed the garden, I said, without turning around: "Au revoir, madame," to which she replied, "Au revoir," with a better accent than mine.

A tall, handsome young man with a mustache: he seemed to lend himself perfectly to wearing an officer's uniform, but in what war could they have possibly fought, as exiles? And in the Varesotto, no less! I was obsessed with the Varesotto, the very name of which sounded to me like the negation of every fantastic hypothesis—and maybe that was why I always added so much of my own fantasy. One fact, in the meantime, had been cleared up: Frenchmen were irrelevant, and even the voices that Felice claimed to hear coming from the ground were merely the memory of overheard conversations between the Kropoffs. The Kropoffs had left abruptly and inexplicably, skipping their final meeting with my grandfather—and what if they had been killed by Felice and buried in the yard? What if those voices were the fruit of his own guilty conscience, a clue that he had revealed to me in the unconscious hope of being found out and punished for his crime? His father, in his version of events, had waged a personal battle against the French—and what if this was a figurative way of representing a family conflict? Maybe the old couple had greatly wronged him, and he had killed them out of revenge: in that case, it was the two old-timers who had subsequently been transformed by Felice's delirious mind into the mysterious entities who possessed the house. In terms of the slugs, they fit perfectly into this psychopathological and fantastical picture, like little Furies sent by the dead to haunt the man whose hands were stained with the blood of his own blood. I had wanted Stevenson, Pushkin? Well, now I had wound up with Aeschylus, and the switch didn't please me in the slightest.

The element that felt literarily extraneous was the Great Rabbit. But why did I necessarily need to think of Lewis Carroll? There were stories by Lovecraft in which a similar character wouldn't have seemed out of place . . . Plus, the Rabbit's eyes had been ripped out, and wasn't there Hoffmann's frightful tale "The Sandman," in which an eerie character roamed about yelling "Eyes here!" as though at a market? At the same time, Felice claimed to have been raised by rabbits and to have spent his childhood among them, and this redirected us to the realm of *The Jungle Book* and *Tarzan* . . . But could I go on like this, grasping at novels and tales? Why did Felice necessarily have to be Lennie? Why did the barrel of slugs need to have once contained amontillado?

I was asking myself these questions, walking up and down the yard, when, not far from the rabbit hutch, I noticed something bright in the grass. I bent down to take a closer look: it was a piece of metal sticking out of the earth, and I had seen it only because in that precise spot the grass was shorter. Pushing aside the dirt, I pulled out the object, and found myself holding a silver teaspoon. A teaspoon? The wee spoon! The instrument of the horrific ocular enucleation! Could it be? It certainly was a strange coincidence for it to be only a few meters from where we kept the rabbits, but . . . but hadn't Felice made it all up? I examined the object more carefully. Could it possibly be Russian? It could. It had no hallmark, but, most importantly, it also didn't bear the number "800," which they'd only started using at the end of the nineteenth century to label silver objects, a fact that therefore proved its antiquity. I waited anxiously for Felice to arrive, and as soon as he did, I showed it to him.

"Japers, the wee spoon!" he exclaimed, without a moment's hesitation.

"Listen here, you didn't lead me to find it on purpose just to scare me, did you?" I pointed to show him the exact spot of my discovery.

"Me! An' it lyin' under the sod for more 'an fif'y years!"

"Then why is it so shiny? Shouldn't it have blackened?"

"Sure 't be shiny, silver, don' ye know?"

"Yes, if you polish it, otherwise it becomes darker—not to mention when it's underground, with all those acids and salts."

"Oh-la-la, now we're chemiss, so?"

"And in your opinion it's that *exact* teaspoon?"

"The one! An' I tell ye this, they're after makin' ye fin' it till they put the fear o' God 'n ye."

"Well, they found the right guy—you know what my motto is: Bugger off ta hell!"

"Min' yerself, Michelin, min' yerself . . ."

"You want to scare me too? Well then, you know what I think? I think that when you were little, you went to play with the rabbits all the time, the way any child would, and there was a particularly big one that you liked more than the rest. Until Mr. Kropoff killed it to eat cacciatore style, which he did without even having the decency to care whether you saw or not, and the part of that horrific scene that stayed seared in your memory was the very moment he took out the animal's eyes with a knife—not with a spoon, but with the same knife he used to kill it. And since Kropoff spoke French, little by little the idea formed in your head that the Great Rabbit had been blinded by the French. There, that's what I think."

"Y'are a quick one, so ye are. Fair play! Fair play t' me Michelín!" and he hawked an unusually powerful gob.

"Felice, where are you going?"

"Goin' home, can't be stayin' 'ere t' listen to this blatherin'! An' I losin' me mem'ry."

"Wait, don't be like that!"

"Michelín."

"I'm listening."

"Sure I hope t' be wrong, I do, but I'd not want 'em to decide to waken th' other—th' other Michelín."

"Why, is he sleeping now?"

"Ay, now he's sleepin', but min' if they gets good an' cross, they can waken 'im."

"And then what will happen?"

"Then ye be goin' asleep, Michelín, an' yerself'll be goin' down b'low."

By the next day, naturally, we had already made up. Perhaps being so forgiving was a shortcoming in a monster, but I wouldn't have wanted it any other way. I decided to further pursue the question of his father's name, seeing as Aurelio actually came from a Neapolitan song. I presented him with a few possibilities, asking him as usual to concentrate with his eyes closed.

"Ivan."

He shook his head.

"You don't have to shake your head, just stay still . . . Alexander."

He was about to shake his head, then stopped himself.

"Sergey. Fyodor. Lev. Anatoly. Pyotr. Vasiliy. Andrey. Vladimir. Nikolai. Mikhail."

At "Mikhail" he gave a start, and raised his hand as if to ask for more time. It would have been funny if his father had the same name as me, although it was also possible that my name was the very thing confusing him.

"So, is it Mikhail?"

"Migh' be."

"Mikhail Kropoff, how does that sound to you?"

"Like Mikhail Strogoff, sure!" Then he laughed, with his eyes kept diligently shut.

"And what would you know about Mikhail Strogoff?" I asked him automatically, without noticing my own arrogance.

"Yer granda used call ye so—me singin' ye 'San Michel' 'ad a Rooster,' an' he callin' ye Michelín Strogoff."

Mikhail Kropoff . . . I couldn't have said why, but it sounded way off the mark . . . Then it occurred to me that Felice was a Latin name—as Latin and as Italian as they come—a name no Russian could have given, much less a Francophone Russian. It therefore must have been his mother who named him that; after all, mothers are the ones who want to give their children auspicious and protective names, not fathers. There was no way a little czarist prick had named his son Felice. If anything, he would have named him Pietro, Nicola, Alessandro, after the greatest and the most atrocious czars . . . I had hit a wall, but needed to find a way around the impasse.

"Felice, what is Russia, for you?" I asked him point-blank.

"Russia? Be a bear, yer big Russian bear."

This was not the fruit of his own imagination, of course. On some occasion he must have heard that cliché, and now he repeated it mechanically, like those individuals who to indicate New York say "the Big Apple," and thus plummet to the very bottom of my disesteem. I can't deny that I was disappointed: my rustic monster, talking like a two-bit journalist! Had he added General Winter, too, I might have pretended we didn't know each other.

"And what is France?"

"France—a slug."

Oh, here he was speaking straight from the heart! A nice and red, insatiable slug! The slug as crystallization of his own madness. For a second, I imagined a crazy painter from the early seventeenth century whom Roberto Longhi dubbed the Master of the Slugs . . .

"Felice, do you think they're good to eat—slugs, I mean?"

"'Em green an' 'em brown ones, ay. 'Em red buggers, no."

"Why not the red ones? Do they have a bite to them? Do they cause stomachaches?" I had in mind what my grandfather had taught me about boletes, and how easy it was to come across the lurid bolete or Satan's bolete.

"Can't be eatin' 'em red ones."

"But if you hate them so much! Why not try sautéing a few?"

"Are y'off yer head? I says it can't be did!"

"But why not? Who decided?"

"Be a mort'l sin."

"Though this doesn't stop you from cutting them in two with your spade."

"Killin's one thing, eatin's another."

"So it's taboo?"

His gaze shifted to express incomprehension.

"I mean, is there a special ban, is that it?"

"Tha' 't be."

"And who imposed it? *They* did?"

"If y'a'ready know th' answer, why ask me?"

"Because I'd like to hear you tell me. Plus, it's not as though you always give me the same answers. You keep introducing new elements that contradict what you've said before."

"An' amn't I losin' me mem'ry?"

"Look, you're not being clever with me, by any chance?"

"'Ow d'ye mean?"

"I mean that you lose your memory when it's convenient for you."

"Ah, tha'd be a gran' thing to do!"

"The name of this town?"

"Nasca."

"The name of my grandfather?"

"Giusepp."

"My grandmother?"

"Uh . . . hol' on . . ."

"Remember, the *lady* of the house . . ."

"The ledy . . . Letissia!"

"Good job. Name of the frothy torrent that flows by the quarry?"

"The Frova."

"The vegetables in our garden, starting from the gate next to the chicken coop and going down?"

"Well . . . Y'ave yer beans, yer green beans . . . t'matoes . . . ehm . . . cucum'ers . . ."

"No, think of the two that rhyme."

"Ah righ', t'matoes, p'tatoes . . . cucum'ers . . ."

"No."

"Aubregines . . . courgitts . . . then yer cucum'ers . . . caross . . . rosemary . . ."

"That's all, everything else is on the other side."

"So I done good, like?"

"Great. Kropovich, Kropchenko, Kropinsky, Kropoff, Kropiyevsky, Kropotkin, Kropovsky, which is right?"

"Kro . . . Kro . . ."

"It's another rhyme. Remember the Dori Ghezzi song, the dance of the steppe—"

"Kasachioff! So mus' be Kropoff!"

"Name of your father?"

"Aur . . . oh damn it ta hell!"

"It's all right, this one you simply don't know."

The municipality of Castelveccana, to which Nasca belonged, had been invented by the Fascist prefecture. As far as anyone could tell, it was comprised of the lakefront from Caldé up to Porto Valtravaglia, though excluding the latter; moving inland, it included, in its first swath, San Pietro and Ronchiano, then, in a second area conventionally called "the valley," Nasca, Saltirana, Ticinallo, and Brezzo di Bedero, and finally, in a third "valley," Sarigo, Domo, Muceno, and Musadino; taken together, these non-valleys officially formed Valtravaglia, one of the valleys of the Tre Valli Varesine cycling race, along with Valcuvia and Valganna. Some people maintained that the municipality stretched all the way up to Sant'Antonio and Arcumeggia, if not to the Cuvignone Pass—but I knew that at least the last of these three fell under the jurisdiction of the Italian Alpine Club of Besozzo. Regardless, a town or residential area with the name of Castelveccana had never existed: I'd been asking questions on the subject for some time, but no one, from my grandfather to the last elderly inhabitant of Musadino, had been able to point to even an old building or ruin that could justify that name. Proof of its nonexistence was the fact that Castelveccana's municipal hall was located right above the village of Caldé, next to the schools. I went there on a sultry August morning, with a letter

97

written by my grandfather that gave me, a minor, permission to conduct cadastral research on his behalf.

The reason for that research? Carmen had said that as far as she could remember, Felice had *always* worked on our property: but if that was really the case, he must have carried out some work—even if not in the full sense of the word—*before* the arrival of the Kropoffs in 1917–18. If, as previously established, he was born around 1910, there were still a few years left unaccounted for, meaning I needed to find out whom the house had belonged to in that period. Unfortunately, after leafing through a dozen or so sets of records, I, as well as the diligent civil servant assisting me, had to acknowledge that the municipality, created in 1923, conserved only documents concerning the current state of things from the time of its foundation on. In fact, our property was first listed as already belonging to Mr. Nicolai Kropoff, born in Minsk in 1873; then, from March 1955, as belonging to Mr. Giuseppe Ferraioli, my grandfather. But why had the local officials at the time made a clean sweep of the preexisting documentation? To free up space, probably; or because the Fascists, despite their Roman rhetoric, couldn't have cared less about the past, and the more they were able to erase, the better.

Equally frustrating was my inquiry into the name Castelveccana. The first document to mention it was the charter for the new municipality itself, signed by the prefect and countersigned by none other than Achille Starace. A shudder, as I read that name—but a shudder without any novelesque pleasure to it, without any Lovecraftian murmur to render things bewitching: only a shudder of disgust. Starace! The prefect was named Carmine Adeodato, whom Felice would have dismissed as a "bleedin' south'ner." Could it be that he had invented it, that godforsaken name of Castelveccana? Where the hell had he found it, in Cesare Cantù? In Bazzoni's *The Castle of Trezzo*? In a bad Walter Scott translation? Castelveccana, what an absurd name for a place that didn't exist!

I was about to leave when I remembered something that must have subliminally struck my retina just as I was beginning to consult the land registers. I asked again for the oldest set of records, and in fact, in volume 104, page 77, number 43 b, sub. 8, lot 1021—that is, our house—there was the following note, squeezed into the margin in pencil: "Ex Dregluss." How was I to interpret this? That an error had been made in the previous registry and subsequently crossed out with an X? That before the Kropoffs, the property had belonged to people with the last name Dregluss?

Naturally, the first person I turned to was Felice.

"Dregluss? Means nothin' t' me."

"Try harder; someone must have been here before the Kropoffs!"

"Ay, 'em rabbiss!"

"And there wasn't someone who bred the rabbits?"

"Som'ne . . . wai' . . . wait ye now . . . som'ne . . . no, am after forgettin' it all."

"But you do remember the Great Rabbit."

"Ay, 'im I do. Dregluss, no."

"What a pain in the ass!"

"Eh, lad, is tha' a way to be talkin' now?"

"You say it all the time yourself, me arse this and me arse that . . ."

Then I returned to the question of Castelveccana, pointing out to him that he was probably a teenager in 1923, and therefore should remember what the area was called before then.

"Nasca."

"Nasca made up its own municipality?"

"Le' me think . . . No, maybe 'twere toge'er wi' Port."

"And Caldé?"

"Dunno nothin' abou' Caldé, an' 'em weeshy folk reared on nothin' but trout."

"But come on, when you all found out that you had become the municipality of Castelveccana, weren't you surprised?"

"An' why be s'prised?"

"Because it was the first time the name was ever mentioned. Does it seem normal to you, to suddenly call a municipality by a name that no one's ever heard before?"

"T'ain't bad, like, Cast'lveccana."

"It's not a question of it sounding good or bad; it's that it was forced, making it an act of violence."

"Vi'lence or no, tha' be the name."

"But you don't have the slightest idea where the name came from?"

"Have me an idea I do, but I ain't tellin' ye."

"And why not?"

"Eh, 'cause, 'cause . . . 'cause it be a 'portant secret, y'understan'? An' tha's enough now, understan'? D'y'understan' or no, for fecksake!"

Every day, he was becoming more irritable and boorish—he who had always been kindness incarnate with me. Was I the one, perhaps, leading him to where I had wanted him from the start, that is, to monstrousness? But what was he trying to cover up? Initially, I had been convinced that he wanted to fight against the passing of time and the malady that he said had plagued all his ancestors; that he wanted to retain his cognitive faculties and actually expand them, to find out more about his father, to move upstream through his anamnesis no matter the cost. Now, on the contrary, he seemed a hunted animal willing to abandon everything so long as he'd be left alone. He was even prepared to let go of his father out of fear of those imaginary beings . . . And what angered me the most was that in order to drop everything, he was prepared to trick me, to mislead me, even to threaten me . . .

Nevertheless, there was no doubting that his fear was authentic. In a Bond film, I had seen James Bond stick a hair over a door gap, so that he'd know whether anyone entered the room while he was gone; well, I did the same with the cellar door, and it revealed that, in spite of my story, Felice never went down to check. So, either he had already known about the barrel full of slugs, or he was so scared that he chose to stay far away.

That night, as had consistently been the case for some time now, I was unable to fall asleep. In my mind I went back over all the names from that day, names of places and names of people: Castelveccana, Minsk, Alexander, Starace, Musadino, Strogoff, Adeodato, Cuvignone, Dregluss . . . At Dregluss, I felt pierced like an insect with a pin and sat bolt upright in my bed, suddenly covered in sweat—for I had just realized that it was an anagram of red slugs.

Ex Dregluss, ex Red Slugs! As if for some reason our plot of land was popularly named after those red slugs, seeing as a long-gone civil servant had added that marginal note as a kind of specification, though misconstruing its form. Was I perhaps to infer that the property had been left vacant, to the point that red slugs and other animals had taken over the lawns and gardens grown wild? In that case, Kropoff would have had to acquire the cadastral unit directly from the state property office; but at least some trace of such a transaction would have been left in the registers. More likely, the property was indeed abandoned, but not without an owner, someone who for years lived far away, without taking care of the place. But if that was true, then how would little Felice have been able to live there "among the rabbits"? Maybe the owner had left a farmhand on the property who bred rabbits all on his own. And, at this point . . . why not come full circle and assume this farmer was Felice's father? Anything but a brilliant dragoon officer, and with no shining saber either! In terms of the slugs, the farmer might have only wanted to look after the rabbits and chickens, and by completely neglecting the vegetable garden had tacitly handed it over to the slugs, who wouldn't have believed their luck in finding a garden they could freely access without risking death . . . But untended, devoured by those mollusks, what kind of vegetable garden could it have possibly been? In less than a year, it inevitably would have been reduced to an underbrush of weeds too hard for those little mouths, and in two years' time it would have become indistinguishable from the brambles and fern thickets that covered every uncultivated area. So why cite the red slugs in that document?

Even granting that the slugs had colonized the property, another problem remained. If old Kropoff had decided as soon as he became the owner to reclaim the vegetable garden, putting his son in charge of its restoration and disinfestation, it would explain why little Felice was left with the impression of a full-fledged crusade fought by young Kropoff; but it meant, too, that at a certain point in his life the little boy substituted his real father with that young Russian . . . Why? Because his father was ugly and the other was handsome? Because his father beat him brutally and the other gave him candies? Because his father killed his beloved rabbit and was never forgiven? Because his father died and the Kropoffs adopted him? And what if, instead of a father, there had been a similarly horrible and hated mother, whom young Kropoff had gotten pregnant? Or worse: what if there never was a young Kropoff to begin with, and the old nobleman from Minsk had been the one to impregnate her? Perhaps for Felice it had been enough to see a portrait of old Kropoff in his youth to deduce that a son existed: then, sure, the boots and saber made sense . . . Nor could I exclude the possibility that he was the natural son of an unknown father, though even then he should have been registered in the parish records under his mother's last name: but what if she had run away from another town precisely to flee shame, without ever officially declaring the birth? This would leave us with a perfectly fatherless child, ready to latch on to the first useful paternal figure he clapped eyes on . . . But . . . but for someone who has never had one—especially if he doesn't have the chance to make comparisons with other children—a father remains an abstract idea, whereas a mother, no matter how early she might die, leaves a physical void, which a little orphan would have to try to fill before ever worrying about a paternal surrogate. Felice, on the other hand, invented for himself a father, and never thought about his mother again, and this was truly strange.

Enough! How many hypotheses had I developed by now, how many useless questions had I put to him, to Carmen, to the parish priest, to my grandfather, to the municipal workers! I had started as a mere mnemonic helper, and look where I had ended up . . . Damnable mnemonic devices . . . One of the most basic practices in mnemonics consists in associating an idea or thing with a number, according to arithmetic, geometric, algebraic, or algorithmic sequences that allow one to automatically configure an exact and invariable picture, in which every element corresponds to a sought-after thing. Ingenious solutions had been devised in past centuries, such as imagining a complex palace of knowledge duly divided into vestibules, atriums, nooks, grand halls and hallways, such that walking through that virtual building was like consulting an encyclopedia; but the mental internalization of that structure was nonetheless realized through numbers. And it doesn't take a great deal of intelligence to understand that any alphanumeric system has to be founded on a defined common language. The simple affirmative word "yes," for example, could be equivalent to 25, because "y" is the twenty-fifth letter of the alphabet; or 3, because it's a three-letter word; or else 25, 5, 19—those being the first and most obvious alphanumeric correspondences. But if I teach these things to someone for whom the word for "yes" is "ay," what do I obtain besides further confusion? Meanwhile, I didn't even have the necessary competence to adopt his dialect as our reference language—assuming that, poetic uses aside, there's any sense to be had in a written dialect. And could I lead him through an imaginary baroque palace, if he had never set foot outside a shabby nowheresville like Nasca? Could I talk of the Tree of Knowledge to a semiliterate man who barely knew how to write his own name?

On top of all this was the unpleasant sensation that, over the last few days, he had been mocking me. That teaspoon, for instance: nothing could rid me of the suspicion that he had buried it himself in order for me to find it. Had he been keeping it in his home? Had he stolen it from my grandmother? Anything was possible. It's true that I hadn't found others like it in our house, but there were so many old stray utensils that this didn't mean a thing. I decided to go on the counterattack: I knew that in our toy closet there was an old doll, so old that no one even remembered to whom it had belonged; and although it had lost some of its clothes and all of its hair, it nonetheless retained two beautiful glass eyes with light-blue irises . . .

"I found them!" I said, as soon as he set foot in our yard.

"Foun' wha' now?"

"The eyes of the Great Rabbit. Look."

I stretched out my open hand, and in it the two glass marbles shimmered like jewels. He opened his eyes wider than I'd ever seen before, filaments of resin stretching between his gaping eyelids. Then he started to tremble.

"Where're y'after fin'in' 'em, poor scoundr'l?"

"In the cellar, where you said."

"An' mad y'are, mad!" He covered his face with his hands as though he did not dare think of what was going to happen next.

"I'm not afraid, you see?"

"Ay, the brav'ry 'f asses!"

"I may be a donkey, but either way I've found them for you, and now we need to interrogate them."

"'Terrogate 'em for wha'?"

"First, to find out who ripped them out of the poor Great Rabbit."

"No, no, I don' want t' know at all!"

"Well, I do—take a look!"

As I said this, I took one of the eyeballs between my fingers and rotated it until I was staring at the pupil, or until the pupil was staring at me. And in the black of the pupil, due to a strange effect of the light reflected therein, I saw not my face but Felice's, who in fact was no longer standing in front of me but at my side. I wanted to believe its verdict: he was the murderer, he had done that heinous thing to the rabbit. I hated him, but before I could turn to express my growing hostility, he had vanished. Had he understood that I had understood? Or had he seen something even more heinous in that eye? Felice: a true monster. And what if the rabbit was a metaphor, onto which his unsound mind had projected the figure of his father? Maybe the young Kropoff had big ears, or was a coward who used to shake with fear like a rabbit. Maybe one day Felice happened to overhear the old man say as much to his descendant. But why, then, would the rabbit be "great," if Felice remembered him as a slender and spruced-up little coward? And if the Great Rabbit actually was old Kropoff himself?

Despairing of wresting any more information from that impossible man, I decided to act on my own, and to start, I planned out two inspections. The first took place in the cellar, and it confirmed what I had expected: the amalgam of slugs and verdigris had become as hard as a rock. However, on the surface, caked like cooled lava, new slugs now crawled unscathed, slugs that therefore couldn't have risen from the earth underneath the barrel. In some way or another, the slime of the deceased slugs must have neutralized the verdigris's poison, which I knew to be deadly both in a solid and in a powdered state. For the moment, I let them continue strolling along, promising myself to drown them in a fresh ration of verdigris if they grew in number.

The second inspection was more hazardous, for, of all places, it had to be conducted in the monster's house.

I waited for him to come out to cut the grass; then I went to his house. I knew that he never locked his front door, so it was almost like passing from one room in our home to another.

I didn't like the first thing I saw one bit. It was a drawing, sketched in chalk on a wardrobe door, depicting a hanged rabbit. But it wasn't the subject that disturbed me; it was the style, identical to that of a child no older than five. I opened the wardrobe: it contained every sort of odd thing, ruffled clothes, little boxes of Bolzano razor blades, a bottle of Floïd aftershave, a thermometer, six or seven issues of *Famiglia Cristiana* and *Cronaca Vera*, a pair of muddy boots, a set of tiny liqueur glasses, a bicycle pump, a jar of brilliantine, a quilt, a pillow covered in yellowish stains, an empty bottle of Amaro Cora, and many other things of that nature. All things of that nature *besides one*: a samovar! An authentic samovar from the turn of the century, by the look of it. Silver, decorated, hallmarked, with an ebony handle, an object that seemed to have come straight from the Hermitage! What was it doing in there? Had the Kropoffs given it to him as a gift? I doubted it. To forgo such a precious and symbolic object for the benefit of a boor who wouldn't have known what to do with it—no, he had more likely stolen it. But why steal it, if not to resell it afterward? Surely a samovar couldn't have held any aesthetic or sentimental value for him. Giving it a shake, I heard a rustling sound: sure enough, inside there was a piece of paper rolled up in a pastry ring, like the paper slips they drew at the town lottery. I pulled it out and read, and what it said, in its apparent simplicity, was painful. On the slip, in a childish handwriting that matched the drawing of the rabbit, a single word was written: "Felicity."

Felice, Felicity. And it was inside an object representing the Kropoffs; in other words, a family. Was that what he longed for, had it always been that—to have a family? His uncertain penmanship made it impossible to date that word, which could have been written fifty years earlier or that very day. The only thing I knew for certain was that the drawing of the rabbit hadn't been there when I came to cover the walls of his room with mementos. But sticking to the question of family: if that really was what haunted him, why hadn't he tried to endear himself to my grandparents? On the contrary, he seemed to take all possible measures to keep his distance: with my grandfather, he communicated in one-word answers that were hardly more than grunts, and I had noticed multiple times that when my grandfather was in the yard reading or looking after the roses, he'd turn right on his heels and postpone his work; in terms of my grandmother, who considered him a genuine brute, he appeared to enjoy frightening her by surprising her from behind, or shaking the bloody pelts of skinned rabbits for her to see. I could have sworn that one time, in the early days, they had invited him over for lunch on some occasion or other, but he had declined. Sure, as far as families went my grandparents weren't anything special, although, at the end of the day, if being an orphan was his original, unhealed wound, he shouldn't have been so picky . . . Especially since the Kropoffs couldn't have been the most likable people in the world. Far from it: a group of Russian exiles who lost everything they had just so they wouldn't have to recognize the Soviets, and fled to the Varesotto... Maybe it was unfair of me to see the Varesotto as the most agonizingly awful point on Planet Earth; maybe if a People's Commissariat had dispossessed me of my white birch trees and my rivulet, I, too, would have hightailed it out of there with a little Romanov family portrait around my neck...

Felice, Felicity... Felicity, Felice... That piece of paper could have been a vow, a desire for happiness, or for eloquence. But had I needed to venture a guess, I would've bet that it was actually a kind of protest, the denunciation of an unfulfilled syllogism, of an etymological betrayal: what, my name is Felice and I'm not happy? My name is Felice and I can't remember the right words? Had he known that the original meaning of Felix was "fertile," would he have been aggrieved not to have any children?

I carried on with my inspection more quickly, knowing that he could come back at any moment. In the drawer of the nightstand I found a broken alarm clock, the kind enclosed in a greenish case; a handkerchief dirty with something that surely hadn't come from a nose; a coupon from *Mickey Mouse Magazine* to attend Rolly Marchi's ski rally on Monte Bondone; a corkscrew; a deck of Piacentine cards bent lengthwise in the usual fashion of countryfolk; and finally, once again, something that left me dumbstruck. Whoever has seen one like it has no need for a description, but for anyone else, visualizing the object is not all that simple. It was one of those secular holy pictures, with a gold-colored base supporting a metallic circle enclosed like a clock face in slightly convex glass; and under the glass, printed on cardboard, there was a photographic montage depicting the men who in the early 1960s were considered the three benefactors of humanity and the guardians of world peace: John F. Kennedy on the left, Pope John XXIII in the center, and Nikita Khrushchev on the right. Two versions were easy enough to come by: in one, the three portraits were each closed in individual oval frames, while in the other, the three men seemed to be literally shoulder to shoulder, with a blue sky behind them in the background. This was one of the knickknacks with the sky, but what left me stunned was what Felice had added to it: for on the upper portion of the glass, so as not to cover the three faces, another piece of paper was glued, a thin and poorly cut strip on which, in that same childish handwriting and without the "h," there was written "Micelin."

After bewilderment, the first thing I felt was gratitude: associating me with those three! Then embarrassment and a sense of inadequacy sank in, for what in the world was I to him, if he inserted me into such company? Or else it was a protective gesture, essentially putting me under the wing of the most powerful men he knew. The first two had died in 1963, so he probably hoped they would protect me from above . . . At the same time, Felice wasn't a believer, and it was strange for someone who didn't believe in the Madonna or the saints to turn to an American president assassinated in Dallas . . . Then I had an intuition: if the paper in the samovar expressed his crippling desire for a family, why couldn't this have the same meaning? What were Kennedy, Khrushchev, and Pope Roncalli, in popular perception, if not a family of the just? Did this photomontage not depict them standing together like three brothers posing for a family photo?

All of this was moving, but terrible too. Terrible for him but also for me, because few things afflict the heart as deeply as discovering how much you are loved by another. Today, now that I've lived more than half a century, nothing has changed— today, as then, if and when it happens, it is a revelation I am not ready to bear. I knew that Felice loved me, but not to such an extent . . . And to think that I had convinced myself over the last few days that he was turning against me . . . Fault after fault, shame upon shame . . . There is no knowledge that does not lead to pain—why, then, had I ever embarked on solving that mystery? Knowing that one is loved is already unbearable, but to find it out in secret is even more obscene than being a voyeur hidden in the bushes . . . I put everything back in the nightstand as I had found it, while I dried my tears with a sleeve; then I ran home as fast as I could.

The following day, I received proof of just how pregnant and binding words were for Felice. Naturally, I had spent a good part of the night seeing that *Micelin* over and over again in my head, without imagining that in the morning I would receive a second helping.

My grandfather had a green Morris Mini which he parked in the space under the hayloft. That morning I decided to wash it and, in so doing, carry out the duties of the cabin boy that I was. Dressed in a bathing suit and equipped with a bucket and sponge, I got to work: work that I hated and yet, being to my great misfortune a perfectionist, conducted with obsessive care until the car looked as though it had come straight from a dealership.

I was just washing the rims of the wheels when Felice walked over to me and said, "Ye see? Yer granda loves ye loads so he does."

"Why?"

"Look 'em tires."

I observed the tire: it was a Michelin. Therefore, according to his brain's laws, if my grandfather had fitted the car with Pirelli or Kleber tires, it would have been a clear sign that he didn't love me. I wondered if this type of fixation had intensified as a result of our mnemonic exercises, or if it was completely autogenous.

"So then, if a man has a daughter named Flavia or Giulietta, he has to get one of those two cars?"

"Course."

"And if he gets another kind?"

"He ain't a good da."

"So your father was good, if he named you Felice."

Before answering, he looked at me suspiciously.

"Eh, me lad . . . givin' names ain't hard, but makin' 'em true."

For a few seconds I simply scrubbed at the rims, so capable was that man of leaving me speechless.

"Tell me this: would you prefer to have been given a different name?"

"O' course! An' not have this felicetay bollix griggin' me!"

And there we had it. Finally, something that seemed to move in the direction of clarification and resolution.

"And if you'd had a son, what would you have liked to name him?"

"Oh . . . have t' be thinkin' o'er tha'."

"Rolando? Sergio?"

"Eh, t'ain't aisy, like . . ."

"Gaetano, Guglielmo, Osvaldo?"

He spat with flamboyant disgust. "Ach, Osvald'—ra'er be dead!"

"Why?"

"Weren't he the bastar' killt Kennedy?"

"Yes, but Oswald was his last name."

"Same thing. Like t' be wringin' his neck wi' me hands like a capon so I would!"

"You know they already killed him? Someone named Ruby saw to it."

"An' good on yer man Ruby! Like t' be shakin' his han'!"

"They killed him too."

"'Oly blazes!"

"Well, for that matter, last year they assassinated Kennedy's brother too."

"No!"

"Oh yeah, a year ago exactly."

"Madness . . . Poor fam'ly, so famous, but wi' shite luck . . ."

Family. There at the heart of it all.

"'Tweren't good for 'em t' be gettin' inta pol'tics, 'em Kennedys . . . Better they was growin' spuds . . ."

"Well, that's for sure . . . But even Julius Caesar wouldn't have been assassinated if he had stuck to cultivating his little plot of land."

"Another 'sassinated? An' 'ow many folk d'ye know is met such an ugly end?"

"Oh, tons . . ."

"Cripes, never thought it so."

"It's an ugly world, Felice. The more you get to know it, the more it'll horrify you."

"An' meself thinkin' all the beaut'ful things o' this worl' was outside Nasca!"

"Where, in France?"

"France can bugger off ta hell!"

"In Germany?"

"Bugger off ta hell, 'em Germans!"

"In Russia?"

I had no doubt that his response would change.

"Don' know Russia . . ."

"Well, you don't know France or Germany either."

"But I known 'em Frensh an' Germans, race o' mangy dogs!"

"But you did know Russians—the Kropoffs."

"'Em Kropoffs was livin' 'ere, an' so they was like from Nasca after a time . . ."

My goodness, this I had not been expecting. A reverse form of adoption . . .

"Tell me something: did they ever come over to see you?"

"Wha' ye mean?"

"If they ever came to see where you lived."

"Ne'er a once, like."

"A regular pair of neighborly Nasca locals, huh? And your father?"

"Me da wha'?"

"Did he ever go into your house?"

He shook his head. "If he did, I fogott'n it."

"And my grandfather?"

"Once when I were taken sick wi' fever, an' he takin' me temp'rature an' givin' me a med'cine till he goes, end o' story."

"Listen, you told me about a grandfather from before: which one did you like more?"

"Chrisomighty, the firs'! But by a mile!"

"And why's that?"

"'Cause the firs' were goin' t' 'ave me sleep in a room upstairs, but this one weren't wantin' it at all."

"He promised it to you, the first one?"

"Promised, no, but I understant it, tha' there were a room jus' for meself."

"And how do you explain it, this change?"

"T'ain't much t' explain: the firs' were alone, the sec'nd were wi' yer nana."

Left on my own, I processed those newly acquired pieces of information. My grandfather comes two or three times, always alone, to see the house and to make agreements with the Kropoffs. Knowing all too well the value of a caretaker and groundskeeper, especially when one is the proprietor of an unheated house that's left shut up all winter, he doesn't exclude the possibility of setting aside a room for Felice, and accidentally slips a hint or two in this regard. Felice deludes himself into thinking he has found the family he always wanted, and he nurtures this dream in the meantime. Then my grandfather returns with my grandmother, who, more puritan than a Quaker and more pious than a novitiate, sees Felice as a kind of brute and satyr who spends his days blaspheming and spitting. Immediately, she vetoes that man entering our home, and, for his own peace of mind, my grandfather indulges her. Thus Felice feels betrayed: the man he had known is no more, he died; in his place another grandfather has illicitly taken over, something akin to a body snatcher. A quite plausible reconstruction of events—too bad that it was undermined by the fact that Felice had claimed that I, too, was double, and that the old me was "sleeping." Had I perhaps betrayed him too? I didn't think so; in fact, I categorically excluded it. Then why had he made me die? And, in his imagination, where was he sleeping, that first me? Underground with the loathed French? In the secret storage room with the three Germans? Or was he inside of me, ready to take back the upper hand? Once again, every step forward was followed by three steps back, while I was being sucked further and further into a vortex of questions.

That night I felt so weary that, while I attempted to fall asleep, I wasn't even surprised to find myself thinking of the reassuring protection of Kennedy and the good pope.

My grandfather was a Republican; not in the anti-monarchical or anti-Francoist sense of the term, but simply because he voted for Ugo La Malfa's party. My grandmother, alas, was a Christian Democrat, but, like half the people who voted for that party, politics didn't matter to her: only the crucifix mattered. Excluding, therefore, my grandmother from all possible dialogue, I was left with my grandfather, whose moderate secularism allowed me to hope for a sufficiently credible assessment of characters such as the Kropoffs, who, for my grandmother, were naturally only fine people who had been oppressed by the horrible Communists. The interview with my grandfather was, nonetheless, a disappointment. Not only did he not wish to speak his mind on the question of the general exodus of Russian nobles, but even in terms of the Kropoffs he remained extremely elusive. Two or three meetings, he maintained, weren't enough to form an opinion, in part because the conversations had revolved exclusively around economic questions; and the last meeting, as I already knew, didn't even take place, because when he arrived the Kropoffs had already moved out. I asked if he'd seen any family members other than the two old folks: no, he had not; besides a woman who must have worked by the hour, and not counting Felice, there hadn't been anyone else. There hadn't been anyone else, or he hadn't *seen* anyone else? He seemed to pretend not to recognize the difference. I then asked if Nicolai Kropoff had mentioned a son: he didn't remember. In the meantime, he was looking at me like a teacher of esotericism glaring at his young disciple for some unforgivable error. That look made me feel like putting up a fight. He had La Malfa? Well, I had two dead Kennedys plus the most likable pope of all time, so he could decide for himself whether such a face-off was in his best interest. I confronted him head-on, asserting that the Russians' sudden flight from Nasca was very suspicious.

"I'd like to see what you'd do, with Stalin's henchmen on your heels."

I recognized the game he was playing: dignify those lazy idlers by turning them into martyrs. But from the little that excellent books and excellent teachers had already taught me at my young age, I knew that Stalin was interested in axing people like Trotsky, while he let ex-czarists do whatever the hell they pleased. In fact, in my automatic antipathy for the Kropoffs, I had almost convinced myself that they themselves were Stalin's spies, and that their flight was due to a suspicion that they had been found out by some genuine, anti-Stalinist Communists.

A new element, in any event, had now come to light: the Kropoffs didn't have servants. It wasn't hard to understand poor Felice's delusion that they had taken him in to be a member of the family who would help around the house . . . Especially since they say that Russians are some of the most hospitable people in the world . . . Whereas if he was hoping to obtain the approval of a Daughter of Charity of Saint Vincent like my grandmother, he was out of luck: help the poor, so long as they stay far away . . . As for me—what could I do? I wasn't even fourteen years old yet; if it had been up to me, Felice would've already gone underground to fight with the French . . . I felt a lawyerlike demon had taken hold of me, and I wasn't going to give up yet: I asked my grandfather if it seemed strange to him that no one knew anything about Felice, not even his last name.

"It happens, in the countryside."

"And what about no one knowing who owned this house before the Fascist era? Do things like that happen too?"

"They can happen."

"And a Fascist prefect randomly making up a new name for a municipality, that can happen too, and with not a *single inhabitant* remembering the previous name?"

"That's life, *tout passe . . .*"

He was answering me in the manner of an old Mafia godfather. I was appalled. *Panta rhei*, the same old crap they teach you in school to get the better of you. Everything flows and nothing stays, you convinced yourself that things were a certain way when, upsy-daisy, they've changed; it's not a scam, it's backed up by the ancients: *panta rhei*, but of course—the maxim that had the power to send me out of my mind. And yet my grandfather had always refused to take the Fascist party card, he had gone as a volunteer doctor to Montenegro to care for those unfortunate souls and had rejected every attempt at corruption, decrying the high-up Montenegrins while attending to the destitute . . . Was that my first grandfather? Did I need to think of him as having died in the war? Either way, I doubted that Felice was privy to that admirable past . . .

"What about after the Kropoffs disappeared, did any mail ever arrive for them?"

"I don't think so."

"Did anyone ever come looking for them, to ask about them?"

"No, never."

I was about to give up. Then my exhaustion latched on to a final foothold.

"The verdigris—Felice used to spray it back then too, right?"

"Yes."

"He told me the Kropoffs made wine, does that sound right to you?"

"Sounds right. You've seen for yourself all those old bottles of must in the cellar."

"Yeah, but setting aside for now that I don't think it's very common to bottle must, did you ever try any of this wine?"

"No, they didn't leave so much as a bottle."

"But what does Felice say? That it was good?"

"Ask him yourself. Aren't you great friends?"

"Well, you know, his memory isn't what it used to be . . ."

"Anyway, making wine was never something that interested me. Too expensive, too much risk."

"Oh right, when there's already Folonari, Zignago . . ."

Folonari and Zignago were two very economical wine brands which, over time, stoked a great deal of ill talk regarding my grandfather's proverbial stinginess. A third, Tavernello, would start to be sold some years later. As a matter of fact, my grandfather had never understood a thing about wines, as became shockingly apparent one famous Christmas when, after receiving an extremely costly bottle of Château Lafite from my uncle Ippolito, he first watered it down, and then, before the disbelieving eyes of all those present, poured into his glass a teaspoon of sugar, stirring it vigorously to make the wine "bubblier" . . .

"Since when are you interested in wine?"

"Look, you're a doctor and you recognize the signs of alcoholism. Does Felice drink a lot?"

"A lot is one way of putting it! Haven't you seen the nose on him? One look at his nose and you know exactly the state his liver is in."

"Why, then, does he tell me that he likes to drink soft drinks, lemon soda, tamarind, barley water . . . ?"

"What a question! Because he's ashamed, isn't he? Now he should even have to go confess to a young boy?"

"But he tells me everything!"

"That's what you believe. Do you think it's easy for an adult to tell a kid he's a drunk?"

"But when does he even drink? There aren't any bottles in his house, and he never goes to the bar."

"He doesn't go to that Bergonzoli joint, but try asking down at the osteria."

"Ah, so you're saying . . ."

"I'm not the one saying it: everyone knows that he's always there drinking."

"At the gelateria?"

"Gelateria, osteria, the only one there is at the end of town."

"And he really drinks that much?"

"Tons. You can't imagine how much."

Why had I pretended not to know what was right in front of everyone's eyes? Out of love, I hoped.

"But did he already drink back when you bought the house?"

"He certainly did, but not as much. It was one of the reasons your grandmother didn't want him to come live here."

Ah, there was my answer. The pious woman. If Felice had been living with a girl out of wedlock, it would have been the same. If he voted for the Italian Communist Party, that would have been the same too. I had no trouble picturing her, my grandmother, embroidering the scarlet letter. And yet never had a single bad word about her come from Felice's mouth: everything was always a matter between men, like in westerns. Even though he knew that she had barred him from living with us, he didn't hold a grudge against her; instead, he had distinguished an earlier grandfather without her from a subsequent grandfather with her.

By the time I walked away from our conversation, I'd been stricken with an unspeakable sadness. The affected diplomacy of my grandfather's responses, the cursed aura that exuded from our house, my entire way of life, all of it made me feel like the loneliest being on earth. My only interlocutor was a poor devil who didn't even know who he was, and I was so desperate to tie myself to someone that, in spite of everything, I continued to see not a creature in need of rescue, but a friend to lean on. And to think that in Hebrew my name meant "Who is like God"! What a farce . . . Michele and Felice . . . For a moment, it seemed to me that the only serious and honest parents were the Spanish and Neapolitans who gave their daughters sorrowful names like Dolores and Addolorata . . . Spain and Naples against France, Germany, Russia, and the Varesotto. Maybe that was my real problem, that I was a southerner living in the north, the horrible north with its little villas and factories! For that matter, my other grandfather, whom I would lose just a few years later, was from Puglia, a fact I was proud of without even knowing why. I'm still proud of it today, only now I understand the reasons.

But I don't want to talk about myself; I need to talk about Felice. Which means, at this point, that I need to talk about wine.

Who could say if alcoholism was another hereditary gift, like the curse of amnesia? What was certain was that Felice felt ashamed, as though he were the only drinker in the world, when it was rather apparent that everyone in Nasca liked to throw down a few, and the women no less than the men. The osteria at the end of town always had one or two patrons seated at the bar, and rarely would anyone exit the general store without a bottle of Folonari or Zignago in their shopping bag—not to mention all the people who made their own wine. I never saw Felice at the osteria when I passed by on my bicycle, but the explanation was simple: he went after dinner, when I no longer stuck my nose outside our front gate.

I had the opportunity to delve deeper into the topic the next morning, when I ran into the parish priest in the middle of the street. As usual, he invited me to spend time at the oratory, a prospect that had always horrified me despite the marvelous foosball tables that went *clack! clack!* all day long. Responding evasively, I then decided to take advantage of the chance encounter and try to find out more; knowing that I was dealing with a priest, I presented the issue in charitable terms, telling him that I didn't know how to help cure Felice of his problem. I was referring to his memory loss, of course, but the priest took for granted that the problem in question was drink. And so he said that there was little one could do, because, every evening, Felice drank abhorrent quantities of wine until he collapsed on the floor; that it nearly always took two people to bring him home and, propping him up under his arms, carry him all the way to his bed; that every attempt to persuade him to practice his vice in greater moderation simply managed to send him into a rage, and on these occasions he shouted that only in wine did he find what he had lost.

I knew that talking about it with the concerned party would not be pretty, but it seemed the only way forward. And so, at the first opportunity, I shifted our conversation toward that delicate topic. He did the dignified thing and didn't deny it, but I could see that he was greatly pained. I asked him why it was that he drank only after dinner.

"'Cause 'f I were drinkin' in the day I'd be no good for workin' an' 'd be gettin' the sack from yer granda."

"I understand."

"An' I don' want ye seein' me like tha' at all."

"The priest told me you say that in wine you find things you've lost. Is that true?"

"True."

"And may I know what?"

"Guess."

I could imagine the right answer, but out of tact I offered two incorrect ones first.

"Youth?"

"Ach, g'wan!"

"Women."

"Bah, divil a one!"

"Your father?"

"Righ' y'are."

125

"And you find him always?"

"'F on'y! Lucky t' be seein' 'im two o' tree times a mont'..."

"And he's always the way you described him: tall, handsome, with a mustache and in uniform?"

"Tha' way, always tha' way."

"And does he tell you anything?"

"Nothin'!"

"But how can that be?"

"Amn't I after tellin' ye nothin'!"

"And do you say anything to him?"

He shook his head.

"So then what do you two do? You just look at one another in silence?"

"There y'are."

"And does he seem happy to see you?"

He shook his head again, keeping his eyes down. Poor Felice, having to get drunk to regain a father who was little more than an Épinal print . . . I needed to change the subject immediately.

"I was wondering, were you the one who used to make the Kropoffs' wine?"

"I used look after the vinyar' an' c'lect the harves' an' smash the grapes. But the wine were his own affair."

"The old man's?"

"Th' oul fella, ay."

"And the must?"

"Tha' too."

"And in your opinion, why did he put it in bottles?"

"Ah, dunno tha'."

"You never asked him?"

"Meself, talkin' wi' th' oul fella? The less ye was talkin' wi' 'im the be'er."

"You know what I'm thinking now?"

He looked at me through the crack between his encrusted eyelids.

"That it's not must in those bottles."

"Ach, the talk 'n ye!"

"You want to bet? Why don't you come down with me to check?"

"Not ev'n 'f I were dead, like."

I therefore went down by myself, took one of those bottles, and brought it to the woodshed. There, we cracked it open with the pointed peen of a hammer, and the presumed must was freed. Having previously filled a little less than half of the bottle, it now formed a solid cylinder, which was considerably heavy to handle. It left brown traces in our hands, as though from rust.

"Ye see? Mus'."

"It kind of smells."

I handed him the solid block, which gave off an ironlike, coppery scent.

"I don't think that's what must smells like, no matter how much time has passed."

"An' righ' y'are—t'ain't mus', no"—and he went pale.

With another whack of the hammer, he broke up part of the cylinder, took a few fragments, and put them in a bucket, pouring a trickle of water on top. Then he shook it. When there was nothing but a dense liquid at the bottom of the bucket, I wetted my fingers and smelled them. I had adventurously wished for the worst? Now I had it.

"Here, you smell it too," I said to Felice, handing him the bucket. He stuck his face in like a horse at a watering hole. Then he reemerged, white and purplish, his mouth agape.

"Be blood, blast it!"

And blood it was. In our cellar, the Kropoffs had left at least twenty half-full bottles of dried blood.

"Blood, Michelín!"

"Yes, blood . . ."

"An' now?"

"First of all, let's not say anything to anyone. Secondly, we'll have to figure out if it's human blood or not."

"Eh, hum'n, can't be! Sure 'll be blood o' rabbiss, pigs, cows . . . Maybe they was lookin' t' make black puddin' . . ."

"Well hold on, didn't they tell you it was must?"

"Ay . . ."

"And would they have needed to lie to you to make black pudding? Think about it!"

"Russian bastar's . . ."

"My grandfather is also convinced it's must, so they lied to him too."

"Think if wi' tha' mus' I were gettin' the notion o' makin' wine . . ."

"We can't discount the possibility that the Kropoffs drank it."

"So 't be true tha' Comm'nis's drinks the blood o' wee 'uns . . ."

"Felice! The Kropoffs weren't Communists, they were czarists!"

"Still Russians."

"As a matter of fact, vampires come from Transylvania, which isn't all that far from Russia . . ."

"Known it afore, ne'er would a' been trustin' 'em at all."

"Anyway, to find out if it's human blood or not, we have to have it analyzed, but I don't know any laboratory; and furthermore, if it's human blood, I don't want to have to justify being in possession of it . . . The only option would be to send my grandfather and have him say the bottles belonged to the Russians, but he'll never do it."

"An' why no?"

"Because he doesn't want any trouble."

"An' so?"

"And so nothing. We'll clean up everything here, and we won't touch another thing in the cellar."

The idea of definitively excluding the cellar from our plans was so pleasing to him that he immediately got to work cleaning the floor, without so much as a word. I, however, was not finished with the cellar, because there was still that barrel.

When, ten minutes later, I pointed my flashlight inside the barrel, I saw that the few slugs still crawling atop that mishmash during my previous inspection were now dead. Apparently, even when melded with all those mollusks and hardened along its outer crust, the verdigris had done its work, the reckless creatures now lying stiffly curled and contorted in the final pose of their agony. I put the lid back: my grandfather almost never went down to the cellar—much less did he go peeking into the barrels—but it was better to play it safe.

That night, while my grandparents were watching one of their usual teledramas, a miniseries starring Aroldo Tieri and Sergio Fantoni, I took a piece of poster board and wrote down, in alphabetical order, the names of all the principal elements in the story as though they were tarot cards. And so I wrote:

Amnesia
The Barrel
The Blood
The Cellar
Death
The Eyes
The Father
The Frenchman

The Garden
The German
The Grandfather
The Grandmother
The Grapes
The House
The Lake
The Lettuce
Memory
The Mother
The Partisan
The Pope
The President
The Priest
The Rabbit
The Russian
The Samovar
The Slug
The Town
The Verdigris
The War
The Wine
The Woodshed

I had left out Felice and myself, but what cards would we be? The Countryman and the Boy? The Drinker and the Child? Or was I supposed to call us by our names, Felice and Michelino? Carmen had been left out too, while it was unclear by what right the Mother had been included. That mother who was only a great mystery—the great mother . . . the grand master . . . the green matter: verdigris . . . vermin grease . . . grant unto the vermin what is the vermin's . . . By playing with words, one always ended up with the same result: nonsense.

I went back over the story's salient points, dividing them according to probability and improbability, plausibility and implausibility; I separated what I'd witnessed from what I'd merely been told; I identified contradictions and conundrums; I established a correspondence table between the transfigurations that had taken place in Felice's mind and the events that might have inspired them; I put on hold in a kind of limbo all the elements about which it was impossible to know anything . . . And yet, in opposition to these good intentions, there was at work in me a spirit of decadence and abandon that made me privilege precisely those things which were the most absurd and mysterious: the eyes of the Great Rabbit, the subterranean muttering of the French, the me "from before," the dragoon officer's uniform—all elements that refused to be rationalized or set aside, and which gripped me with the power of their impenetrable charm . . .

I realized that I was only going to founder in the midst of that schema, and that, as a preventive measure, I was better off examining one element at a time. I chose to start with the slugs, because someone must have put them in that barrel. Without worrying about the why—a question exceeding my capabilities for the time being—I decided to focus on the how. And puzzling my wits for an answer, I found the point where I could have been led astray: it was when I had seen those new slugs crawling on top of the upper crust and had assumed that they couldn't have risen from the bottom like the rest, and that someone must have brought them there instead. And the reason I could have been mistaken was that the staves were sufficiently slack and disconnected as to easily leave an interspace between the wood and the vile slug paste, along which the last moribund mollusks could have crept upward. So, using a rod as a lever, after a few attempts I successfully tipped the barrel over: upon hitting the ground, it broke apart into a tangle of staves and rusted iron, but its contents remained intact. Seen from above, it looked like congealed fish soup, a bloodcurdling thing; but more frightening still was the confirmation of what I had speculated. For, in the floor of the cellar, right where that barrel had stood for who knows how many decades, there now stared up at me a gaping black hole, irregularly shaped and as big as a fist in diameter. Poking at the sides of the hole with a small stick, I realized that the cellar had no flooring whatsoever but stood directly on the earth. Hence, from that sort of mole hole the slugs had come up in droves, perhaps called up by something or fleeing some thing, and, running into the rotten wooden bottom, had easily broken through and filled that cask to the brim. At this point, Felice would have surely brought up the buried French: just in case, I ran to the woodshed and prepared a little verdigris in a bucket, and then, after making sure that no one would see me, I went back down and poured it into the hole, which drank it up thirstily. Naturally, I expected the sound of wailing to rise up from the bowels of the earth, and just as naturally convinced myself I'd heard it.

I could trick Felice about anything, so long as it wasn't his verdigris. If a single clump was missing, he'd notice even before looking inside the sack. Therefore, when he came to water the garden, I informed him of the latest developments in the cellar. Contrary to my expectations, he reacted with muted disapproval, and soon I understood why: the fact that nothing had happened to me despite my recklessness transformed me in his eyes into an individual endowed with special powers or special privileges. But I was not to push too far, because push and push and "they" would start to get tired of my insolence . . .

"Do you mean the French, when you say 'they'?"

"No."

"Why don't you tell me once and for all who they are? Maybe I can help you."

"'Cause . . . 'cause 'f I tell ye who . . . if I tell ye, they'll be killin' meself too."

"What do you mean, you *too*? Who else have they killed?"

"'Em undergroun', the Frensh."

"And when was that?"

"Eh, such a long time 'go, wouldn't 'member ev'n if me mem'ry weren't banjaxed."

"But the ones who killed the Frenchmen, were they Germans?"

He shook his head as though I were way off.

"Russians?"

A light shake of the head echoed the previous one, as if to more frugally communicate its message.

"Italians?"

He nodded—grave and solemn.

"Italians?!"

"Ay, 'talian as can be."

"Alive or dead?"

"Ach, some 'live, some dead . . ."

"But who were they—people from Nasca?"

"From Nasca, from Sarigh, Mucen, Domm, Musadin . . ."

Never since the start of everything had I felt as close to the truth as at that moment, even if so much verbal expressiveness and such precision on the part of Felice seemed in their own right a mystery.

"It sounds as though you're talking about a band of partisan soldiers, you realize that?"

Pouting his lips, he made the face of someone flaunting complete indifference.

"But why would the partisans massacre the French?"

"Eh, who knows . . ."

The usual Felice was back, shielded behind his defenses. To get back on his good side, I told him that if he really wanted to, he could knock off a few slugs: while we were talking, I had seen three or four creeping among the chicory, and I'd noticed that he had seen them too. There was no need to tell him twice. After hurrying to the woodshed to grab his spade, he proceeded without further delay with his surgical dissection.

"Do you feel better now?"

"B'gob!" and he hawked a big one on the nearest cadaver.

"Hey, watch it! You know that chicory is for eating?"

He doubled over with laughter. He looked so happy that, with no ulterior motive, I gave him unlimited permission to slaughter. He almost kissed my hand with gratitude. Poor Felice . . .

Over the next few days, I noticed how systematic he was in the elimination of those red slugs. The other slug species, meanwhile, could roam about the vegetable garden and even nibble on a little lettuce without running the slightest risk. The rotting corpses of the red slugs didn't seem to bother them in the slightest, leading me to reflect on how distinctive from one another such animals can be, the very animals we humans, starting with our language, consider to be the same.

Too bad the Frenchmen underground weren't like their slugs, for once reduced to skeletons, they'd no longer be distinguishable from Germans or Russians. And this was what I wanted to do now: find one of those Frenchmen.

The most suitable spot was behind the larch, amid the clumps of knotweed: there, no one would be able to see me at work. The safest time was right after dinner, when it was not yet dark out, with Felice at the osteria and my grandparents in front of the television: that evening's miniseries was with Marina Malfatti and Andrea Giordana, so the coast would be clear. I took a lighter spade than the one Felice used as a guillotine, and started to dig. The ground was soft, just as it had always been, but I hadn't accounted for the tangled roots that radiated out in every direction from the larch, the spruce, and the blackthorn. I therefore used shears, too, and by the time it had grown dark my hole was still laughably shallow. I covered everything with broken branches and weeds, and got back to work the following evening, under the televised auspices of Orso Maria Guerrini and Rossella Falk. That evening, there was even a crescent moon in the clear sky, so if I put my back into it, there was hope I might find something before the show ended. Instead, I once again had to suspend my excavation: this meant the third night would be the charm, while Loretta Goggi was pretending to be a boy in the miniseries adaptation of *The Black Arrow*.

When, if not then, on a Stevensonian evening, could I have cast my eyes on the white gleaming of a femur in the moonlight?

Heedless of the blisters lacerating me, I dug all around it with my hands and, driven nearly into a frenzy, did not stop until the skeleton was completely uncovered. Still intact, it lay composed, like a sleeping man. I ran into the house to get a brush: Arnoldo Foà's booming voice was speechifying, I still had a little time left. With the bristles, I delicately brushed the earth from the bones, and only at the end, when I came to the skull, did I discover the cause of death: the sole sign of violence along the whole skeleton was a small hole in the neck. So, an execution had taken place. "They" had condemned to death and killed "this one."

Is there any need for me to describe what I did the following evenings, night after night for a dozen or so days? I don't know how I would have managed without Giulio Bosetti and Paola Pitagora, Alberto Lionello and Umberto Orsini, Ilaria Occhini and Adalberto María Merli, Ubaldo Lay and Massimo Serato, but in the end—an end conservatively preestablished in order not to excavate insufficiently hidden areas of the lawn—I could count fifteen adult male skeletons. Some revealed the same bullet hole in the neck with one or two extra perforations in the temple, but others had many more holes in their scapulae, their sternums, their femurs, as though they had been mowed down by machine-gun fire. They must have been executed and then buried naked, because, as much as I looked, I did not find a single strip of clothing or uniform, not a belt buckle, button, military flash, piece of leather—nothing whatsoever. And, naturally, no weapons either. Were they more Germans executed by the partisans? Partisans killed by the Germans? I didn't have a single solitary fact to go by. There was only Felice's version, according to which they were French. Could it be that a French detachment had run into a group of Germans while the latter was retreating, and a gunfight had ensued? If so, some must have been French and some German, but who had then gone to the trouble of burying them in such turbulent circumstances? Certainly not the survivors, whichever side they were on. Italians then, if for no other reason than to avoid the spread of disease: but, in that case, why so much secrecy? Why, at the war's end, had they not made news of the event public and moved the remains to a more suitable location? Why did the people who knew keep quiet? Felice himself had said that some of the individuals responsible for that massacre were still alive, and that they were locals, from the "valley." I was certain that Carmen was among those who knew, but I was even more certain that she wouldn't let so much as a word slip. Maybe I could trick her into talking by setting a kind of trap, but to do this I'd need to mention Felice, and would thereby get him into trouble. Fifteen dead men: who could say how many more would be uncovered by digging up the whole yard . . . Fifteen men on the dead man's chest, it didn't get more Stevenson than that! Yes, maybe I was a lucky boy, maybe it was the reward for my stubborn determination to stay a child and never grow up; even now, this desire hasn't left me—just imagine how I felt it then, at the age of thirteen and a half . . .

The slugs ate memories . . . Unfortunately, this fixation was only true in Felice's mind, otherwise the battle would have been noble and beautiful, worthy of one of those sci-fi movies I liked so much, *The Invasion of the Mnemophagi*, *The Gastropods from Outer Space* . . . Even more absurd was the claim that the French were the ones sending them, apparently to exact revenge . . . The idea of vengeance, however, wasn't to be cast aside: if Felice knew something about the massacre, if he had witnessed or actually taken part in those killings, his own sense of guilt could plausibly make him experience his memory loss as a deserved form of punishment . . .

The potential number of bodies buried on our property led me to imagine the most anti-scientific thing I could think of, namely, that this breed of slugs had come into existence only then, becoming so fat and so red after switching from lettuce to the blood and the flesh of all those fallen soldiers . . . Anti-scientific? Well, yes, it was anti-scientific, even if . . . But no, what nonsense, to eat the bodies the slugs would've needed to move underground like moles, and this didn't seem possible to me . . . Ultimately, I decided I had to find out for myself: I took a red slug of considerable size, dug up a bit of dirt, and buried it underneath. After an hour, I came back to check: the slug had died of suffocation, without moving a single millimeter.

In all this, the figure still missing in action was the father. I was becoming increasingly convinced that it couldn't have been the young Kropoff: even if he had immediately impregnated a commoner after arriving, at the earliest, in 1917, that would then make his son only fifty or so years old, too young to be Felice. It's true that Felice's life had everything in it to make an individual look older than his age: between childhood abandonment and trauma, hereditary illnesses, a face devastated by smallpox and birthmarks, a mouthful of missing teeth, backbreaking work from which he never took a vacation, alcohol abuse, and his habit of handling verdigris without any protection, there was enough to age a man ten years—yet that young Russian didn't convince me . . . His elegant uniform, for example, was clearly inspired by some image in a magazine, since it was unthinkable for an exile to strut around in czarist garb in a town where, if there weren't any Stalinist assassins around, there were nonetheless plenty of partisans. Here, too, it was easy to argue that Felice's father could have shown him an older photograph of himself, but why would he have shown it to him at all, if he had excluded the boy from his life? Felice could have seen the photo sitting on a mantle, my imaginary devil's advocate retorted, but would it have been prudent for those exiles to exhibit such a telling image of their past to the first craftsman or municipal messenger who happened to enter their home? The information I possessed was limited, but all of it suggested that the Kropoffs were very scared and kept their guard up—and wasn't their son the man who used to shake with fear like a rabbit? So, by the transitive property established by Felice's mental confusion between word, image, and thing, to exclude the young Kropoff's uniform meant excluding the young Kropoff himself: a harsh method, but I had no others at my disposal. To convince me once and for all, and to shut that one door out of many, I tried my best to imagine Felice as a peasant in Tolstoy or as one of Gogol's "souls," but I couldn't: no, there was nothing Russian about him, even if back then, to me, Russians were all just like Gagarin . . .

If I was going to be completely consistent, eliminating the young Kropoff also meant the elimination of the father—of any father. The stubbornness with which Felice described him shining with frogging and spurs was made possible by a void: had there been an alternative—one from the Varesotto—a conflict would have arisen, each layer contaminating the other. Instead, this alternative didn't exist; there was nothing, not even the ghost of a shudder. His mother, too, was a void, but . . . How had I not thought of it before? I had been foolish, so incredibly foolish!

Two voids, yes, but there was still one fully present thing. There was a house.

As far as anyone could remember, Felice had always lived in that house of his. Was he already living on his own when the Kropoffs arrived? Either way, his house must have belonged to someone back then, and if no alterations had been made, as with our plot, then the Fascist administration's land registers ought to have preserved the owner's name. *Ought* to! Rabid Fascist futurism surely could not allow itself to lose sight of a single obscure element from the past, for it was about giving continuity, about tradition enduring . . .

Convincing my grandfather to give me his written consent again was no easy task, and only after I had spun a whole monstrous web of falsehoods did he finally hand it over. At the municipal hall they treated me with some suspicion, but they gave me what I wanted. I examined the oldest cadastral map of Nasca, dating back to 1923; after pinpointing Felice's unit, I wrote down the reference number, then looked in the registers and was shocked by what I found. The only owner appeared to be a certain Marisa Bianchini, called the Dreg Lass; a little cross in front of the name attested to her death. "Dreg lass," not Dregluss! I asked again for the set of records that included our house and carefully reconsidered that annotation: sure enough, what I had thought was a "u" could have easily been a sloppily written "a," while the manner in which it was squeezed into the margin explained why I had read it as a single word . . . I had lost a nice anagram, but in exchange I had gained a possible mother, a mother who cut across both cadastral units . . .

I returned to the parish priest, and after promising that I'd start frequenting the oratory, I asked him to take out the parish records once again. He gave a huff as he did so, I think out of commiseration with my grandfather. If she was his mother, if Felice was closer to sixty than to fifty, and if the fact that she hadn't given him a last name meant that she was very young when she gave birth to him, then she must have been born between 1890 and 1895. Out of a kind of pity, I started by looking at the earliest year, and I was right to start there, because under the date of February 8, 1891, I found: "Today, at 7 o'clock in the morning, Marisa Angela Noemi was born to Alfredo Bianchini and Marta Baruffaldi."

Marisa . . . If I wasn't misremembering, Marisa was also the first woman Felice said he had ever been with . . . It could have been a coincidence—or maybe it wasn't, and he had innocently named his mother as the "first woman" in his life . . . Regardless, he didn't remember a thing about that mother, and I feared that by talking to him about her, my story would automatically become his truth . . . Marisa, called the Dreg Lass—why? For a purplish mark on her face which she passed on to her son, and which I myself had always thought of as resembling wine sediment? Was it possible that the Kropoffs had bought the house from her, a poor girl who hadn't even been able to give her own last name to her baby? And why was there not a single sign that pointed to her in Felice's home, not a portrait, a basket of threads and buttons, a hairbrush, a dress, a necklace? Who had enacted that purge, and why? As always, the more progress I made, the more questions seemed to open out fanlike before me. My latest discoveries from birth and property records were at least as valuable as the fifteen skeletons, if not more so, but I was nonetheless at a dead end.

Not long before dinner, Felice came to feed the chickens. While accompanying him in his task, I asked if he had always lived in his current home.

"Always."

"Are you sure?"

"T'ain't somethin' a body forgehs, his home."

"But you forgot your mother," I pointed out, with shocking cruelty. Unsurprisingly, he didn't respond.

"You don't have any memories of you two together in that home?"

"No. Not in tha' one there, an' not 'n any other neither."

"Listen, that purplish mark on your face . . . have you ever met someone similar, someone who looked like you?"

"Blazes 've I seen 'em! Luìs, Franceschín, an' ev'n yer man the m'chanic in Ronchian, wha's his name? Ay, Rossini."

It was too easy, but it was still an invitation I could not refuse.

"Rossini? Like the musician."

He gave a sort of indecipherable grunt.

"The one with Figaro. You know, Figaro, Figaro, Fiiigaa-rooo . . ."

"Ah, tha' one."

"That one, yes. Do you know that, to tease him, they used to call him Bianchini?"

Another grunt, while I wanted to sink straight into the ground out of shame.

"An' why so?"

"Rossini, Bianchini—red, white: it's a play on words."

"Ah."

"But do you get it?"

"T'ain't much t' be gettin', y'ask me."

I had sunk so low for nothing. But at this point it was too late to turn back.

"It's not an ugly last name, Bianchini. In fact, I like it more than Rossini."

"Sure I'd be preferin' Verdín, Bluín, Magentín . . ." Then he laughed so hard he frightened the chickens. I wondered if he was having fun at my expense, and not for the first time.

"In any case, as far as people with marks on their faces go, you remember only men, if I've understood correctly. No women?"

He froze with his fist in midair, right as he was about to throw the feed to the chickens. He stayed motionless for what felt like an eternity, then he scattered the seeds, rubbed his hands against his thighs, and, closing the chicken coop, looked me in the eyes.

"Ye mean to be tellin' me somethin', don' ye?"

"It's true, I do."

"Then ou' wi' it!"

"It's just that I don't know if you're ready."

"So 't be somethin' awful, like."

"No, not at all, but . . ."

"But wha'?"

I didn't know myself. Then, as tactfully as I possibly could, I told him about his mother, about that woman who was *almost certainly* his mother.

"Marisa Bianchini . . . Marisa Bianchini . . . Marisa Bianchini . . ." He was mechanically repeating that name as if to give it shape and reality, but I saw that his litany wasn't working. "Marisa Bianchini . . . the Dreg Lass . . . an' so y'are after askin' me if I known som'ne wi' a dreggy mark on 'em like meself?"

"Yes, because it's a detail that could make you remember her . . . and because it could be hereditary . . ."

"Ah beaut'ful! From me da I get losin' me mem'ry, an' from me ma 'em dregs on me brocky mug!"

"Make up your mind: weren't the slugs of the French the ones who were eating your memories?"

"Oh, boyo, ye'd not be actin' cheeky now? 'Cause I ain't los' all me witses yet!"

Terrifying, he seemed to me. And it was a relief. I would have liked for him to grab a pitchfork and chase after me, because not only did I feel a great deal of nostalgia for my monster, but I also needed him for practical reasons, so that I could forge ahead with him in my investigation. With him it was more fun, a lot more fun. But how was I to tell him that I'd found the skeletons? I would save this information for last, and only if it turned out to be truly indispensable.

I tried to calm him down; by now I had become a perfect sycophant: "What's the word for barley water?"

"Barley water. Wha' kin' o' question is tha'?"

"I wanted to see if you'd fall for it. What year is it?"

"Nie . . . ni'eteen . . . sixty . . . sixty-tree!"

"No, that's the year Kennedy was assassinated."

"Ah, righ', poor hoor . . . So 'twere . . . ni'eteen sixty-eight!"

"That's when they killed his brother."

"Shite for luck, tha' fam'ly . . . Sixty-nine, so."

"Right. Name of my grandmother?"

"Lady Letissia!"

"Great job!"

And at that, like a worm I crawled away, leaving him to gloat.

Two days later, I was once again in his home. Pretending to pick at random, I pointed to the samovar and invited him to touch it.

"Do you know what this is?"

"One time I were knowin' it—now no."

"It's for making tea."

"Ah. Don' like it, tay. An' ye'd be wantin' a big whassit the like o' this?"

"They use it in Russia, or at least they used to."

"'Em Russians, jus' look wha' class o' junk."

"But it's also a decorative item, sometimes they're even worth a lot of money."

"An' this one 'ere, 'ow much she wort'?"

"If you don't know yourself . . . Do you not remember where it came from?"

"'Twere b'longin' to the Kropoffs."

I didn't expect him to name them so easily. So he couldn't have stolen it from them.

"They gave it to you as a gift?"

"Gaves it . . . gaves it . . ."

He froze like a machine that had jammed. He was close to remembering something, but that very proximity must have overheated his brain.

"There's no rush. Keep touching it, squeeze it with both hands."

He silently obeyed, his eyes closed. By the look of his whitened knuckles, he was squeezing it as though he wanted to wring out its secrets by force. After some time had passed, he started to speak in a near whisper.

"The contrac' . . . 'member a contrac', but ye couldn't be signin' it, there wasn't the bob for 't."

"What contract?"

"I were sellin' 'em somethin', to the Russians, now I don' 'member: were somethin' . . . somethin' . . . any'ow, they was owin' me money yet . . . An' so th' oul fella brings me insi' the house, an' he tellin' me to take somethin' dear, somethin' to me likin' he says, till we's square an' all an' can be signin' the contrac' . . . Go lookin' roun' an' th' on'y thing I like be this thingsit, ask how much for 't, a fortunc says hc. Soon said's done an' we signin' an' meself bringin' home this 'ere beas', for I weren't knowin' then 'twas for makin' bleedin' tay, like."

I looked more closely at the samovar. Now that I knew how things had unfolded, it no longer seemed all that valuable: the silver could have been nickel (the infamous "German silver"), and the ebony, any old wood painted black . . . But what could possibly have been the traded object, for which, on top of money, they had needed to add a material possession, albeit an over-valued one? I asked Felice if he still remembered how much money we were talking about.

"D'ye know yerself? An' me neither! If they was givin' me our own bob, but wi' tha' money o' theirs, who'd unterstan' a thing?"

"What do you mean? What did they give you?"

"Russian money, wha' else?"

"Rubles?"

"Ye bes' be havin' a gander yerself." And from the shelf above his sink, he took down a tin of Due Vecchi cocoa.

"You mean you still have it, after all these years?"

He opened the tin: inside was a wad of rolled-up rubles, all ten-ruble notes.

"Couldn't be spendin' 'em now could ye? T'ain't good roun' 'ere, tha' tender."

"But you could have gone to the bank and exchanged it, or demanded the Kropoffs do it!"

"Sure look . . ."

"And you really have no memory of what it is you sold them?"

"No."

Then, suddenly, I had a painful illumination. I prayed that it wasn't true, but I knew it was. Ex Dreg Lass.

"Felice, it wouldn't happen to have been our house, would it?"

"The house, wha' an eejit, yeez's house—how 'm I after forgettin' a thing like tha'?"

An old three-story house full of antique furniture, a two-and-a-half-acre yard with tall standing trees, seven acres of fruit orchards, two vegetable gardens, a hayloft, an outbuilding for storage, a rabbit hutch, a woodshed, a chicken coop, a perimeter wall, a walkway paved with river stones—the Kropoffs had taken all of this for that roll of grimy rubles and a piece of junk for making tea! For a moment I daydreamed of being a KGB agent, with those three swindlers on their knees in front of me, waiting for the coup de grâce . . . I borrowed one of the bills and ran to my grandfather. Pretending I had found it inside one of the few Russian books the Kropoffs had left in the library, I asked him how much it might be worth, and after consulting a treatise on numismatics and a book on the history of the Russian revolution, he told me that the ruble had continually suffered tumultuous vicissitudes and fluctuations in value, and that in around 1913, for instance, a hundred rubles were worth roughly three hundred lire, which corresponded to two million lire in 1969, and that during the war the ruble's value dropped by a third before it lost ninety percent of its remaining value after the fall of the czar in 1917; that the new Soviet ruble thus came to be in the wake of a vertiginous devaluation, at the same time that the old czarist rubles experienced a corresponding increase in value on the black market and outside Russia . . . I stopped him there and ran off with my sheet of notes: if the Kropoffs had left with their pockets full of czarist currency, maybe the amount they paid Felice wasn't so negligible after all. For that matter, how could they have brought Soviet currency with them? Nor did I remember seeing the hammer and sickle on those banknotes . . .

I had Felice hand the tin back to me and pulled out a bill. It didn't have the hammer and sickle, though what it did have was a near joke for a date: October 1917 . . . A ruble that was no longer czarist, because Nikolai Romanov had abdicated in March, and not yet Soviet, because the new rubles didn't appear until 1918 . . . So the Kropoffs had waited until the last minute to leave Russia; they surely held on to their old rubles, but, for everything they sold at the eleventh hour, they had to accept those limbic bills, wastepaper to palm off later on gullible fools like Felice. I counted the banknotes—there were twenty—then did the math and concluded that those two hundred rubles weren't currently worth any more than 150,000 lire. Our house and everything else, for the measly price of 150,000 lire and a samovar! I would never drink another drop of tea for as long as I lived.

"But why? Why? Why didn't you try to find out more, why didn't you ask for someone's help?"

I could have strangled him. He shrugged.

"Don't tell me because you needed money, seeing as you never spent it."

He shrugged his shoulders even higher. I still wanted to strangle him, though also to squeeze him in the most affectionate hug in the world.

"Your mother was already dead, wasn't she?" If she had been alive, she never would have let someone rip her off like that. Not her.

"Forgott'n everythin' abou' me ma. But . . ."

"But?"

"But I 'member the contrac' wi' 'em Russians, an' doin' 't on me own an' wi' no one else—an' after bringin' the sammover home, I were on me lonesome."

Blasted Kropoffs! Stinking czarist bastards! Not only had they come to further taint an already godforsaken land, but they had snatched an entire property for peanuts by tricking a poor soul! Prince Myshkin was nothing in comparison—here, purity had been violated, childish innocence raped . . . He had been tricked, swindled, duped! How old had he been at the time? An orphan, not yet ten years old, who had never known his father and had just lost his mother, an outcast without a last name in a war-torn country, maybe just a few months after the Battle of Caporetto, in a town where there were no men because they were all at the front: for the Kropoffs it must have been like taking candy from a baby . . . One could only guess how many signs of mental imbalance Felice had already shown, to encourage them in their loathsome usurpation . . .

And then he worked under them for years! From 1917 or 1918 until 1955, when they disappeared immediately after selling everything to my grandfather . . . I could only imagine how little they must have paid him, with the excuse that he was a minor . . . Maybe they only gave him some fruit and vegetables and a few eggs, on rare occasions a rabbit . . . Poor child! And then poor young adult, and then poor man! And when my grandfather became his employer, still he hoped to be welcomed back into a home that had once been his! But he had probably already forgotten that fact years earlier, for it was becoming increasingly clear to me that his illness was much older than he had first led me to believe. Yes, he had asked me for help because he was losing his memory, but he had been losing it for half a century . . .

I, meanwhile, needed to start to take care and keep a mental overview of all the elements in the story, from the confirmed facts to Felice's more or less plausible accounts, to my own hypotheses—because only in keeping everything together could I hope to discern the false from the true, and to arrive at a decent conclusion. The epiphany about the mother had reduced, and maybe even erased, the figure of the father; what remained firmly ensconced in the center of the general picture, on the other hand, were the slugs. According to the zoological manuals, the *Arion rufus* could grow to 15 cm in length: however, I, with my own eyes, had seen specimens that were 20 cm long and, in the barrel, even a few that looked to be 22 or 23 cm. In other words, veritable monsters; monsters that seemed to have elected our garden as their homeland. My experiment with the dirt had proved that they couldn't move underground, or rather, that they couldn't move by *digging*: but what if they had found preexisting galleries and tunnels? If moles had left at their disposal a network of passages connecting the French graveyard and our cellar, then the *Arion rufus* could have fed on the bodies for years, becoming bigger and redder in just a few generations . . . A local variant, the *Arion rufus naschensis* . . .

But a further experiment was needed before I could believe in this narrative, and so I conducted it. From the fridge, I took half a slice of bloody liver and laid it in the vegetable garden, close to the lettuce. Right away, three slugs, intent on eating the tender hearts of the heads of lettuce, abandoned the greens to make their way toward the liver, their tentacles stretched outward like bulls' horns; before they even reached it, other slugs also began to throng from every direction. In an instant the meat was completely covered by those darting, quivering critters, whose champing suction produced a horrible squeaking sound. A few seconds more, and the slugs broke apart, slowly returning to their heads of lettuce: where I had laid the liver, there remained only a damp stain thoroughly soaked with slime . . . Carnivorous slugs! A discovery that could fill thirty pages of *Scientific American*! What I had just seen at work were the great-grandchildren of the slugs that had picked clean the bones of countless Frenchmen, assuming they really were French . . . That ancestral nourishment had modified their genes and their habits, and in some way or another Felice must have known this: otherwise, why so much zeal in killing them, while sparing the other species? But what he did not seem to realize was that if those slugs were French, it wasn't for their geographic origin, but for what they had eaten . . .

Yet another experiment concerned our house. If it had belonged to the Dreg Lass, then Felice must have lived in it at least during the first years of his childhood. As soon as my grandparents went to Luino to do some grocery shopping, I took him by the hand and led him through the whole building. There were at least eight bedrooms; in each, he looked around, closed his eyes, sniffed the air, opened his eyes and touched the chests of drawers, the nightstands, and the slats of the shutters, sat on the edge of the bed, stroked the wrought-iron coils of the headboards, closed his eyes again to concentrate . . . and every time it was a no, he had never slept in that room. He had never slept in any of the rooms, and he was dead sure of it. Which meant . . . ? Which meant that he had always lived in the little cubbyhole where he currently lived—always! When I asked him once again if he really was sure, he nearly lost his temper.

"Michelín," he said, as we came back out into the yard.

"Yes?"

"An' me da?"

"What do you mean?"

"Ye tol' me the name o' me ma, but I can't be seein' her . . . Me da I can see a' times, but he can't be foun' at all, an' ye don't ev'n know his name."

"Felice, you have to get used to the idea that your father never existed, in the sense that . . . in the sense that you never knew him—you see what I'm trying to say? Otherwise, he would have left you his last name, whereas you don't even have your mother's . . ."

"An' why can I be seein' 'im if I never known 'im?"

"I think . . . Maybe I'm wrong, but I think the figure who appears in your mind every so often corresponds to what your mother used to tell you when you were little. It was like a fairy tale, understand? That's why you imagine him as tall and hand-some, in a magnificent uniform, because it's how your mother described him to you."

"'Tweren't the trut', like?"

"I really don't think so."

"But 'en, why tell me such bollix?"

"Because your mother loved you."

"An' so?"

"And so she gave you the father that every boy would like to have."

"But if he weren't tha' da there, 'twere be'er somethin' less pretty t' be 'maginin.'"

An unassailable observation. I would have felt the same way; I, too, in the absence of a father, would have preferred for him to be described to me as a disgusting being, so that I'd actually thank my lucky stars that I'd been spared . . . But I wasn't a mother, and even if I put myself in a mother's shoes, I couldn't be too sure about it. What a story . . . And they say that "what ifs" will get you nowhere . . . Now that I can see how much harm Hegelianism has done to humanity, I know that the most beautiful stories are all made of ifs . . . The poor Dreg Lass, if she had known the pain her son would reap from the image of that dragoon shimmering with glory . . . The idea of Felice chasing after that phantom for more than half a century was heartbreaking, I couldn't accept it. But telling him now that his father was a lowlife who had skipped town as soon as he'd knocked up his mother was maybe even worse—what was I to do? I was a young boy, inexperienced in the ways of the world, and I couldn't ask anyone for advice! Had our ages been inverted, I would have told him that I was his father, I would have squeezed him against my chest and covered him in kisses, but this was a dream I couldn't even start to bring to life . . .

I spent a sleepless night haunted by the thought of the Dreg Lass. With that name, she sounded like a witch burned at the stake, and yet she must have been a great woman . . . Not in the eyes of priests, of course, if she couldn't even give her last name to her baby . . . I tried to imagine her: a young unmarried woman gets pregnant, in a small, religiously bigoted town, a kind of scarlet letter situation . . . it's such a scandal that the parish priest at the time refuses to baptize that child of sin, in fact he doesn't even record the birth . . . the child soon shows signs of mental frailty, strengthening among the townsfolk the idea of sin and of divine punishment . . . and so mother and son live increasingly isolated on their land, until one day, when the child is no older than eight or nine, his mother dies . . . for a few months the boy stays on his own, living off the produce in the garden while becoming increasingly wild, then those elegant Russian nobles arrive in town . . . one way or another, they find out about the situation concerning that wild boy and decide to take advantage of it, and for a fistful of rubles and a useless samovar, they buy his whole property, everything except the outbuilding, where the child has grown up . . . then they immediately have him start working for them, treating him as a slave . . . The young Kropoff has a mustache, and sometimes, in his mental confusion, the boy takes him for his father . . . Unlike his parents, the young man travels, disappearing for long periods of time, and this absence seems almost purposely made to be filled with the image of the dragoon . . . As the years pass, however, the young Kropoff grows old and fat, he no longer has his beautiful mustache and his black hair, so that whenever Felice sees him again he finds it increasingly difficult to recognize his father in him, until he no longer recognizes him at all, and the dragoon goes back to being the ghost he once was . . .

Everything fit together quite well, as a matter of fact. Too bad this account left out the corpses in the yard, the bottled blood, the Kropoffs' sudden disappearance, the eyes of the Great Rabbit, and a barrel teeming with a new species of meat-eating slugs.

On January 29, 1964, I was having dinner at my grandparents' apartment in Milan. I had turned eight a little more than a month earlier. At a certain point, they announced on the news that Alan Ladd had died that day.

"Would you look at that," my grandfather said.

"And so young too," my grandmother added.

"Who's Alan Ladd?" I asked.

"You'll see him soon enough," my grandfather said, because they had just informed the viewers that, in remembrance of the actor, there would be a change in that night's programming—instead of the scheduled miniseries with Tino Buazzelli and Salvo Randone, they would show the tale of that lonesome rider who saved the whole valley: *Shane*.

That evening I saw one of the most beautiful films of my life, a film that I would rewatch many times over, finding it more devastating and perfect each time. But I watched it, then, with a special kind of anguish: because the life of Shane, continually hanging by a thread, was nevertheless protected by an assurance that the film would have a happy ending, while in real life he had passed away only a few hours earlier . . . Maybe it was due in part to the cruelty of that initial viewing that I fell in love with Shane just like little Joey, with whom

I unabashedly identified even though he was as blond as a Swede.

On July 6, 1972, like every other summer, I was instead in Nasca. That evening, when they announced on the news that Brandon de Wilde had died in a car accident, my grandparents were the ones to ask who he was, and it was my turn, while I tried not to cry, to explain that Brandon de Wilde, who had died that day at the age of thirty, was Joey. In fact, the news anchor punctually informed the viewers that, in remembrance of him, the scheduled miniseries with Ave Ninchi and the Giuffré brothers would be replaced by *Shane*. And this time it was I, in the role of Joey, who was aware of having just died.

In that summer of 1969, which would go down in history as the summer of the slugs, two days after my last conversation with Felice, I had a dream about him. I was Joey and he was Shane. A Shane identical in every way to the original Shane, but for a purplish birthmark on his face.

"Howdy, kid," he said, getting off his horse.

"Shane!" I shouted joyfully.

"Shh, you'll wake your parents."

"You came back!"

"Yes, but not for long. I have to tell you something, then I got to be going on again."

"Why, Shane, why can't you stay?"

"Because my place isn't here. One day you'll understand." And he ruffled the hair on my head, while his pistols shimmered in the moonlight.

"But you still have to teach me to shoot!"

"You know that your mother is against it."

"But if we do it in secret?"

"Another time, Joey."

"Shane, did you kill many others?"

"I didn't come here to talk to you about that, Joey."

"What is it you have to tell me?"

"Do you remember the pastures out west, where I brought you on my horse?"

"How could I forget, Shane?"

"An ugly thing happened up that way, a long time ago."

"What?"

"If I tell you, will you promise you'll never go there on your own?"

"I promise, Shane."

"There are many dead buried there, more than you can even imagine."

"Did you kill them?"

"No, I only helped bury them."

"But who were they?"

"Indians, who had come down from the highlands in search of buffalo."

"And who killed them?"

"Bad people, desperados, bandits . . . The Indians were lured into a trap and then mercilessly slaughtered."

"But why did you help them bury the dead?"

"I was in a state of shock from all that bloodshed, I didn't know what to do . . . They handed me a shovel, and I obeyed."

"Shane?"

"Yes?"

"Why did you say that I can never go there on my own?"

"Because strange things can be heard up that way, voices . . ."

"Voices?"

"The voices of the dead. Didn't you know that Indians go on talking to one another underground?"

"No."

"Well, now you know."

"Shane?"

"Yes?"

"Can I tell my ma and pa?"

"No, it's a secret between the two of us."

"Okay."

"Now I have to go. Goodbye, Joey."

"No, wait, stay a little while longer!"

"I can't. I have to go."

"Shane!"

"Take care of yourself, kid."

"Shane!"

"Bye, Joey."

"Shane! Shane! Shaaaane!"

But just how ugly was he? I tried to imagine him without small-pox craters, without spots and without warts, without encrusted eyelashes and with a less lumpy and spongelike nose, but he remained ugly all the same. There was something shapeless about his face, as if it had been hurriedly molded with Play-Doh: his mouth, in particular, resembled a wound with no lips—lips that upon closer examination owed their ambiguous perceptibility simply to their color, that purple which looked added on like lipstick. And then there was the vertical scar that ran down from his eye to his mouth, and which crinkled all over when he laughed . . . Actually, I had never asked him how he had gotten that scar. I went into the woodshed to ask him, but what I saw made me forget my question. Bent over the tub, he was diluting verdigris in water and stirring with a stick.

"What are you doing?"

"Have ye no eyes on ye? The verd'gris."

"Yes, but why?"

"T' be leckin' 'em grapes wi' it, ye know tha.'"

"But you've already sprayed them with it twice. That's enough for this summer."

"Twice so?"

"Oh yeah, it's already the twentieth of August."

"Cripes, an' me thinkin' I'd t' be sprayin' it still . . ."

"When in fact you don't . . ."

"Ach, sure 'en 't'll be comin' in handy 'gainst en'mies."

"You mean the slugs?"

"Slugs, Frensh, Russians, Germans, th' 'ole lot 'f 'em!"

"And Italians?"

"Whist! Now I tol' ye some 'em's still livin' . . ."

"All the more reason to spray them with verdigris."

"He's one t' be talkin', the wee lad! Sure he has a swaggerin' tongue an' 'imself a pup on'y."

Most of them were dead . . . some still alive . . . though all of them were people from the area . . . Was he talking about Fascists or partisans? With the partisans he had collaborated at least once, when he helped kill the three Germans, along with Giuàn—dead—and Carmen—still alive . . . Was it possible that he was afraid of that woman? He had never talked about the Fascists. What an exhausting man: I had come to ask about his scar, only to interrogate him instead about the verdigris, while now a question about Fascists had sprung up all on its own.

"Felice, you've never told me what you thought of Fascism."

"Can be tellin' ye aisy, like: shite."

I heaved a sigh of relief, because I hadn't felt the least bit optimistic on this point. Although, unsurprisingly, what he added right after deprived his answer of a good deal of its significance.

"'Em Comm'nis's is shite too, but the bigges' shite o' all is 'em Crishian Democrass . . . On'y Americans do I be likin' at all . . ."

As far as I knew, American soldiers had never made it to the Varesotto to hand out chocolates and cigarettes, yet I believed I knew the reason for that predilection.

"You like Americans because of Kennedy, right? The war doesn't have anything to do with it."

"Poor hoor, tha' Kennedy. Good on ye, lad."

"But I was under the impression that you liked Khrushchev, too . . ."

He shot me a suspicious glance.

"They were friends, Kennedy and Khrushchev . . ."

"Ach . . . I heard tell 'em Comm'nis's killt 'im, Kennedy . . ."

"Actually, it's much more likely that Fascists did it."

"Why, they're in America too, 'em Fascis's?"

"Are they ever! You know that Oswald shot Kennedy because he considered him a friend of the Russians?"

"Unb'lievable . . . An' so we're needin' enough verd'gris t' fill all o' Lake Maggior' . . . Think 'ow beaut'ful, sprayin' all tha' verd'gris on 'em, an' when y'are after finishin' the job y'are lef' wi' a worl' wi' no Fascis's, no slugs, an' no Frensh—blazes 'ow beaut'ful!"

The Fascists, the slugs, and the French: the absurd juxtaposition of these categories within a single sequence all but enthralled me. I would have listened to him for hours when he talked like that. And when, many years later, I read Borges, I'd be reminded of those associations and affirmations on more than one occasion.

I then asked him about his scar. Lowering his voice as though to share a dangerous secret, he told me that when they eliminated the three Germans, one of them had slashed his face with a chipped piece of brick, and that if Carmen hadn't stuck an awl in his neck, the Kraut would have tried to slash him again. Then, without even realizing the trap I was laying for him, I asked why, instead of hiding the bodies in the storage room where someone could find them, they hadn't buried them in the yard. The answer was surprising.

"Ye couldn't be, no."

"Why?"

"Carmen weren't wantin' it, an' Giuàn neither."

"I see, but why?"

"They was sayin' ye can't be mixin' flour an' shite."

"Flour and shite?"

"Be a way o' sayin' two things can't be goin' toge'er an' they bein' so diff'rent, like."

"Different in the sense that one is good and the other bad? Is that what you mean?"

"There y'are."

"So if the three Germans were the excrement, then under the yard there must have been the flour . . ."

"Righ'."

"Meaning the bodies of good people . . ."

"Dunno if they was good, jus' tha' they was killt."

"And they were French."

"Frensh, ay."

"The ones that chitchat underground."

"An' all a cheep-cheep an' chap-chap, worse 'an lasses a' market!"

"Do you know how many of them there were?"

"Loads, but loads I says . . . Lookit, I'd not want to be 'sageratin', but I do b'lieve there was more 'an forty of 'em."

I had found fifteen. Considering the size of the area I had dug up in relation to the rest of the yard, the numbers seemed to add up. Forty skeletons! Under the lawn where I had walked and lain down thousands of times! And how many generations of *Arion rufus* could forty skeletons feed? *Cheep-cheep* and *chap-chap* they went, in French . . . And all the while he had been there to listen . . . Did he *want* to listen, or was he haunted by those voices? It wasn't clear to me. Why was he convinced that they were the ones stealing his thoughts? After all, he had helped bury them, not kill them . . . At some point in his life—or in his mind—something bad connected to France must have occurred, something that transitively spread to those poor dead people and those monstrous slugs . . . The Kropoffs spoke French, but was that enough to definitively associate France with evil? No, because two essential conditions were missing: that they spoke in French even when talking to him, and that he was aware that they had ripped him off and consequently hated them for it . . .

I convinced him to pour all of that precious verdigris into two big empty bins, and while he was busy doing this, I went back to the house to retrieve my collection of Kropoffian objects. I waited until he had finished and washed and dried his hands, then I again handed him that little vase for a single flower which seemed to have evoked Gallic words in him. He squeezed it, fondled it, pressed it against his temple, even gave it a lick: nothing. No French and no Russian. And nothing from the other objects either, which we again went through one by one. We had almost finished, when he realized that one of his spades, the light one I had used to excavate the skeletons, was not in its usual place.

"Wha' the . . ." he said only, and he went to hang it on the rack. Oh no, I thought in a panic—what if he asks me if I took it, and why? What if he guesses what I needed it for?

"Parbleu!" he exclaimed, right as he grabbed it by the handle. "Voilà un grand tas de morts . . ."

"Can you repeat that?" I asked, my voice coming out choked.

"Eh? Repea' wha'?"

"What you just said. But you'll have to pick up that spade again."

He did as I asked, but he didn't repeat a thing. I said goodbye to him, and brought the bag of items back to the house. I had to surrender to what was evidently the truth: the objects weren't the things unleashing energy; rather, I was conditioning and influencing myself and, as a result, telepathically influencing him . . . Yes, my fear that he would find out what I had been up to with his spade was so intense and so focused that it reached his mind, and since the subject of my excavation had been the French, by some mysterious selective mechanism it was not the spade or the soil or the skeletons that hit his neurons: it was the French language, in the form into which my mind had bent it at that moment . . . A case of psychic ventriloquism. I would think, and he would give sonic body to my thoughts—a prospect that was nothing short of obscene. I preferred to imagine that my psychic energy was first transferred to the object in question, before passing from it to his fingertips and to his nerves, all the way up to his brain, but I knew I was kidding myself; I knew that the objects were bypassed in the direct dialogue between our minds . . .

And I, too, then: how many times had I had an idea that actually came from him? How many times had I *been* him?

His memory was deteriorating ever more rapidly. The very day after I had found him preparing the verdigris, a regrettable thing came to pass: having confused the stale bread for the rabbits with the poison-laced bread for the mice, Felice found himself responsible for the deaths of seven rabbits. He couldn't forgive himself, he kept crying and repeating that he didn't understand how after so many years he could confuse "'em loafs" . . . I convinced him to tell my grandfather that the rabbits had fallen prey to a new kind of disease, and the story ended there. The day after that, I once again found him at work after dinner.

"What are you doing at this hour of the evening? Shouldn't you be at the osteria?"

"Ay, an' coddin' y'are."

He was convinced it was morning, and I had to show him that it was almost dark out to send him on his way.

The following night, too, he was in our yard, but for a different reason. He had been at the osteria, where he had seen something on television that distressed him and sent him running to our house: proof that Carmen and I were scheming behind his back! I tried to figure out what in the world he could have seen.

"On the telly, durin' the carousel . . . an' y'are seein' a cheeky fella wi' a 'tache an' hat on 'im, big like this, an' he wi' a name like yers, 'Mighel I be, an' Mighel I still be!' An' this fella goin' to a wee lass, Carmencita, ye see, an' Pierin, he says t' me she were the same as yer one named Carmen, eh, ye see?!"

He was so worked up that he confused me as well, and it took me a little while to piece together what had happened. Miguel was a character who appeared in the commercials for Talmone cookies, along with El Merendero; Carmencita, meanwhile, appeared in the Paulista coffee ads, accompanied by a mysterious caballero; what had provoked the mix-up was the rhyme between "Merendero" and "caballero," and especially the similarity between the respective Hispano-Venetian apothegms, "*Miguel son mi*" and "*Bambina, quell'om son mi.*" It wasn't easy to make him understand that he had only seen an advertisement for a cookie featuring a Mexican cartoon character and then another for a brand of coffee, and that he had nothing to worry about. However, I could see he still wasn't completely convinced.

"What did you see right after those ads?"

"Nothin', 'cause I'm leppin' straight 'ere."

"Right before them, then."

"Uh . . . le' me think . . . ay, the tale o' that oul fella says he were wrong too, for he never gave Linetti brillanty a go . . ."

"Cesare Polacco: Inspector Rock! You see, don't you? One commercial coming right after the other, like in a merry-go-round—that's why the program is called *Carosello.*"

In this manner, amid white lies and minor ruses, we slowly approached summer's end. I looked at our house and felt I was seeing Felice's memory, not only because in a fabled time it had been his, but because it was full of holes and cracks, with a leaky roof and damp stains that caused the plaster to blacken and bubble, woodworm-eaten furniture and handles that broke off in your hand, shutters whose slats came out of their frame and stayed slanted, doors on which the paint was slowly chipping away, a perimeter wall that was crumbling thanks to the roots of creepers, old prints that curved under the glass of their frames and housed in their corners the cocoons of larvae destined never to hatch, iron railings reduced to a bunch of rust and held together purely by repeated layers of chrome and greenish paint, increasingly large areas of the fruit garden overrun with black locust and bamboo, trees whose topmost branches had not been trimmed in years . . . The main cause of all this was obviously my grandfather's stinginess, but it was also the idea, which deep down I was the first to share, that the countryside was by definition a place of neglect and decay, of mold and spiderwebs, a place where we city dwellers merely scratched the surface for a few months a year, but which over the long time frame of its truth, in the quiet autumns and the even quieter winters, slowly yet meticulously progressed toward its own destruction: a realm of larvae, of spiders, of owls, of woodworms and woodpeckers, an intimately dark and damp place—sodden, in fact—a place both poetic and rotten.

I was a young boy, with all the extenuating circumstances boyhood entails, but I found it scandalous that my grandparents weren't the slightest bit interested in knowing the history of that house. They never missed one of Edmondo Bernacca's weather forecasts for the coming days (the horrid millibars!), but the past, even when it concerned the character and the spirit of their own home, held no importance for them . . . At the end of the day, they, in their own distinct way, were not all that different from Felice, who knew Linetti brilliantine but didn't have a clue what Fascism was; who kept the little icon of Kennedy, Khrushchev, and the pope but didn't know the faces of his own parents . . .

But there was another analogy between that poor man's head and our house: the presence of certain memories that corresponded to certain events that had occurred in certain places,

places like the hidden storage room behind the dismantled bed at the side of the hayloft, places like the rich earth that lay under the lawn . . . In both cases, these places and memories housed bodies: was it possible that this was all the past granted us, dead people or ghosts? The executed or the disappeared?

Not daring to talk to him about the Frenchmen, I asked Felice to show me the secret room again. First it was a hard no, then vacillation, then, finally, he wanted to know why. I explained to him that the first time I had potentially missed some details that could prove useful in piecing together one of the many shattered segments of his life. He hesitated some more; then he spat and said, "Ach, fine."

While I was waiting in the hayloft for him to turn the key, I considered once again how strange it was that in the midst of his disintegrating memory he had still remembered where the key was hidden, that first time he brought me there: according to him, in fact, he hadn't gone back in there since 1945. Then I remembered that, for a certain period of time, he had insistently referred to his father as "the key" to explaining everything . . . Was there a link between the key to the room and that metaphor? It was possible, as long as he had still identified young Kropoff as his father in '45, something that wasn't very likely, because at that point the young man was no longer all that young . . . But even supposing that he had, what connection could that Russian have had to the three Germans? And to the partisans? Assuming that he was in Nasca at the time and not off somewhere else, that stinking false key . . . In any case, the two old-timers had surely been home, and must have heard something. Did they hole up, scared, or did they go outside to look? Did they question Felice? I imagined the two sleazy czarists crouching by a window: they see six people go up in the hayloft, Felice along with two other locals and three Germans in uniform, they hear shouting, then they see only the three locals come down ... When they are sure that everyone has left, they go into the hayloft and find nothing, they move on to the adjacent room and find nothing, they go back and search under the hay but, once again, nothing ... Could they possibly not suspect and look for a secret door? Could two worms like them run the risk of the Gestapo or the SS discovering those three bodies on their property? They had duped Felice and taken his house from him—could they really not find a way to make him talk? He had been a child then, that was true, but how many times thereafter did they see signs of his psychological frailty? Instead, they don't do a thing; they keep those corpses on their property for another ten years, until they sell their house and land and outbuildings to my grandfather, outbuildings that include the hayloft ... Who would sell a piece of property with three dead people on it? Was this why they ran off at the last minute? They really must have been confident that they couldn't be tracked down, but wouldn't it have been easier just to get rid of those bodies? Ten years was enough time to search, they could have inspected the hayloft and the little room inch by inch, but instead they simply left everything alone ... Could the truth be plain and simple, namely, that they were stupid? Or that not only had they not seen the partisans go up or come down, but they hadn't heard anything either, because they were old and deaf? Voilà, I could truly congratulate myself: from a single episode, I had unfurled a whole array of dilemmas, an insoluble polylemma.

Then he arrived with the key. I helped him move the pieces of the bed and, while he fiddled with the lock, mentally repeated to myself that I shouldn't be afraid, shouldn't be afraid, shouldn't be afraid: because, actually, it was an adventure.

This time I was the one who held the flashlight. Crouching down next to the skeletons, I illuminated and examined them from up close. One of the three was smaller in stature, substantially so. Before dismay could get the upper hand, I started to unbutton the jacket.

"Wha're ye doin' now? 'S it mad y'are?"

"Shhh, hold the flashlight."

Underneath the perfectly conserved jacket (military cloth—cloth from the frigging Reich!), the other fabrics had more or less dissolved, as though they had taken part in the body's decay, with only a few filaments still stuck to the bones. I removed the jackets from the other two skeletons, and saw that the same thing had happened: the uniform had held up, whereas what had once been between it and the skin had gone the way of flesh. The possibilities were twofold: either the Nazi textile industry put all of its care into the outer uniforms while neglecting shirts and undergarments, or underneath their jackets the three of them had been wearing civilian clothes ... Ruminating on this, while Felice shifted the beam of light from one skeleton to the next as if to make sure they didn't pull any tricks, I realized something else: the first skeleton was not only smaller, but had thinner bones too. I finished undressing them, which confirmed that, underneath the pants and boots of all three, no fabric had lasted. The thin-boned skeleton also had a differently shaped pelvis, a shape I didn't need to look up in my grandfather's medical books to recognize as female.

"Felice, didn't you say that they were three men?"

"Tree fellas, ay."

"This one here's a woman."

"Ah, g'wan ta hell outa tha' . . ."

"I'm telling you, it's a woman. Look at the ankle bones, look at the wrist bones . . ."

"I 'member tree fellas."

"Well then, that means that the woman was dressed as a man. Did they have military caps on?"

Before he could try to remember, I slipped the flashlight out from his hand and pointed it in every direction, until I saw a cap, and then another. Eventually, under one of the skeletons' scapula, I spotted a third. A woman could cut her hair, plant a cap on her head and lower the brim, wear a uniform over her clothes, throw on boots several sizes too big—it didn't take much. And at night, in the midst of so much excitement . . . That he had believed it didn't surprise me one bit, though it seemed strange that Carmen's discerning eye had fallen for it . . .

"Michelín."

"Yes?"

"Was tree fellas we killt. Wha'd we want t' be killin' women for?"

What a hardheaded man . . . Did he want proof? I knew what to look for. I slid the flashlight between the bones of that skeleton until I found, in the whitish dust, the clasp of a brassiere.

"Do you know what this is?"

"A wee hook."

"And what do women hook behind their backs?"

"Brazeers."

"And what is a brassiere for?"

"For hol'in' up bress."

"Now are you convinced?"

"'Oly blazes, but he had bress so!"

We closed and covered the entrance as before. While we did this, he didn't stop muttering to himself: "Bress . . . an' who'd b'lieve it, a Kraut wi' bress . . . an' bress he had sure . . ."

Once I was alone again, I updated my tortured summary. Two men and a woman: the Kropoffs! Having been Nazi collaborators, as well as accomplices in the massacre of the French, after the Germans are defeated they hurriedly join the retreating soldiers, from whom they borrow three uniforms. Something, however, goes awry, and the partisans catch and execute them. End of story. But . . . but! But then, who sold the property to my grandfather ten years later? Someone pretending to be a Kropoff, evidently, which would explain their sudden disappearance following the sale. But who could have taken the place of the Russians for a decade, in a little town where everyone knew each other? And it wasn't just a single person, but three people: two permanent residents and another sporadic one . . . with Felice living next door and working for them *every day*! Here, once again, I narrowed the possibilities down to two: either the susceptibility of his weak psyche was such that anyone could convince him of anything, or he knew everything. But if he knew everything, then he was bound to know that his new employers knew too; for if they didn't, why would they pretend to be the Kropoffs? And with what guarantee that the Russians wouldn't come back to reclaim a property that was legally theirs . . . So, if he knew and the impersonators knew, they were accomplices, and what better suspects than the people who were already his accomplices in the killing of the real Kropoffs? Giuàn and

Carmen, and maybe one or two other partisans from the surrounding areas . . . a kind of cooperative that managed our house for a decade. But why? To use it as an arsenal, in case war broke out again, or as a refuge for ex-partisans, should the new government reveal persecutory tendencies? And what about the rest of Nasca? Most of the men had met their end fighting the Germans or had been rounded up and shot by the SS. Giuàn and Carmen must have held considerable sway over their neighbors, then, and it wouldn't have taken much to convince the older people to keep quiet, if only out of hatred for the Nazis and those three traitors . . . In terms of young children and anyone born afterward, they had never met the Kropoffs, while the house would have remained shut up, the front gate never opening onto its yard . . .

One thing was certain: whether he once knew or not, *now* Felice no longer knew a thing, because the good faith with which he insisted on the male sex of that skeleton was undeniable. Certainly, his capacity for mental repression was prodigious, seeing as another one of those skeletons belonged to the man he'd imagined for years was his father, the false dragoon, who wasn't named Aurelio but maybe Mikhail, like me and like the Mexican cartoon character from *Carosello* . . . Losing one's memory was one thing, suppressing memories was another, and I had the impression that here it was a case of the latter . . . What if his mother, too, had been suppressed, Marisa Bianchini, known as the Dreg Lass . . . And the house? No, not the house; I was almost certain that he had truly forgotten ever being its owner . . . At the same time, he knew where the rubles were, and he remembered the whole scene with the contract perfectly, but the manner in which that story had come to light suggested it was an isolated memory detached from others, a sort of mnestic monad, solitarily fluttering through the increasingly empty spaces of his brain . . . I wondered whether the partisans were aware that the Kropoffs had cheated Felice. Probably—because even if he never said a word about it, the contract kept by the Kropoffs would have turned up sooner or later; I was sure of this, because if the partisans hadn't found it, then I would have, as I obsessively explored that house summer after summer, inspecting even its most obscure recesses. If that's how things had unfolded, justice would have called for the partisans to give the house back to Felice, but how could they be sure that he'd be able to keep up the act? So, that was why the grounds were in such a pitiable state when my grandfather purchased the property, and why there was hardly anything left of a vegetable garden: green beans and cucumbers were the last thing on the minds of the former partisans, and what Felice grew and bred, he grew and bred only for his personal consumption.

If the virtual owners only set foot in the house to conduct their dealings, and so that people would be seen inside it from a distance, then, effectively, the sole protagonist of that theater was him, my monster . . . He and all those Frenchmen underground, and the slugs . . . If I had guessed the truth, and the Kropoffs had been in cahoots with the Germans, it meant the pact was in the interest of both parties, czarists and Nazis . . . The latter didn't dispossess or deport the former, and the former helped the latter as spies, providing logistical support . . . In that case, they had almost certainly had a hand in murdering the French . . . What had Shane said? "Lured into a trap," that was it. The Russians must have offered a safe haven to a band of French soldiers, after which they notified the SS Oberführer . . . I imagined the scene in a horrified rapture, the Russians prattling away in their fluent French as they offer something to drink and eat, the winks, the jokes at the expense of the goddamned Boches . . . They're capable of dissolving a drug in the wine, they make sure that they only serve each other from the countermarked bottle, and with every glass the French become increasingly incapacitated, one of them is already snoring on the table . . . Then they give the signal, the SS arrive, the French are brought down to the cellar, most of them can't even stand up straight and end up rolling down the stairs . . . In the cellar, they have them take off all their clothes so that no military flashes or tags will be found later, then they kill them one by one with a shot aimed at the head, some take it in the nape of the neck, others in the temple, only a few have the energy to react but they get mowed down in a barrage of gunfire . . . Upstairs, meanwhile, the two old Russians clear the table, maybe their son is with them too . . . They are removing any leftovers that could still be good for another meal, scraping them off the plates, when the Oberführer enters the kitchen, clicking his heels, a few blunt orders: bury them in the garden, clean the cellar, burn the clothes, *Schnell!* What, not a single German is staying to help them? The Oberführer doesn't even reply, another click of the heels, an about-turn, and he's gone.

And Felice?

All of those bodies to haul off and bury, and with only two of them to do it, three at most—they'll never manage. But could they disobey the Oberführer? Ultimately, they're left with no choice but to ask for help from that wild man, who, after copious libations, is sleeping in his cubbyhole. What do they tell him? They clearly tell him that those dead men are French, otherwise the mania of that French murmuring would never have spread through the obscure meanders of his brain's circumvolutions . . . They tell him that the Germans arrived and—*ta-ta-ta-ta!*—a bloodbath, *pauvres garçons* . . . Maybe the idea of French soldiers reawakens his mother's old fairy tales about the heroic dragoon, and that's why he agrees to work like a dog all night to bury the dead . . . But then why does he attribute that slaughter to people from the area, to Italians, "'talian as can be"? Maybe the Kropoffs didn't mention the Germans, fearing their collusion would be exposed: but then why would the partisans execute them? Could Carmen and Giuàn possibly implicate him in exacting punishment without explaining the reasons to him? And why "the blazes" would he get it into his head that the French were stealing his memories by using those deadly slugs, just as they had previously done to his father? This, truly, was the question to knock over my fantastical house of cards . . . Why all that Francophobia? Nothing in my grandfather's books connected the *Arion rufus* back to France, but for Felice those big red slugs were nothing more and nothing less than French slugs . . . Was there any chance that he had drawn a link between that species' abnormal development and its diet of flesh and blood? An ignorant rural laborer, an alcoholic who had been losing his memory for years, a mentally unstable individual twisting whichever way the wind blew, having an intuition worthy of Darwin or Mendel? It was a little too much. No, something must have happened in his own life to give rise, in an indirect and convoluted manner, to that hatred: hatred for the French and hatred for those slugs . . . Was it a story that his mother used to tell him about the French? It seemed unlikely to me . . . My grandfather? Even more unlikely, since communication between the two of them was limited to the bare essentials. Something he had seen on the television? Bah! And then, what about the slugs? Plus, there was still that bottled blood passed off as must, and it was anyone's guess what the Nazis could possibly have had to do with that . . .

It was just past midnight. I couldn't fall asleep, and from my grandparents' room I heard positive remarks being made about that night's miniseries with Gianrico Tedeschi and Carla Gravina. When, finally, they stopped talking and all was silent, I became convinced that my intuition was right. I had established that, in some cases, I had telepathically influenced Felice, and it followed that the reverse dynamic could not be ruled out either: hadn't we both already grappled a sufficient amount with the principles of transitivity and reciprocity? Therefore, the next day, as soon as Felice walked over to the rabbit hutch, I tore him away from his work and made him sit next to me on the bench under the grape arbor.

"Felice, now we're going to do an experiment. We'll hold hands and both close our eyes. Then you have to think of something that has to do with France."

He looked at me as though trying to figure out if I was making fun of him.

"Preferably something from long ago, from when you were young."

"France, when I were a lad . . ."

We got into position, and I ordered every fiber of my being to assume a passive state. I kept my eyes shut so tight that my face muscles hurt, and in the dark I saw psychedelic shapes slowly moving about.

Then I saw a vulva. Or rather, I saw something that in the absence of any experience I believed I could identify as a vulva. It lasted a second, then the darkness swept everything away. Convulsively, I kept my eyelids sealed while holding Felice's hand. I don't know which of the two of us was sweating more. I could feel his concentration, as when one feels oncoming rain; then a voice cut through the darkness. It was speaking in Italian, but with a strong French accent. And it was a woman's voice. "Pa grav," the voice said, "you know ow many men eet appens to? Come, don't make zat sad face, shin up, no one as died . . ." Then nothing more reached me, nothing but a wave of unspeakable suffering . . . Images followed—but what do I mean, images? They were more like wraiths of violence, curses, furniture smashed into pieces, and for a moment I thought of letting go of that hand . . . But I held on and faced what was now an outpouring of pain and rage jumbled into one, until suddenly I heard that voice again: "Derty batar," it said, "regard vot you ave done, if you don't go I call zee police, you understand? Such a fuss because your villy eez soff like a *limace*—ow do you say, ah, wee, a zlug . . ." Then the transmission's violence exceeded our capabilities, and we both let go of the other's hand at the same instant: each of us giving a shudder, each of us hiding his face in the crook of his arm.

I didn't know anything about the topic, but I could guess that it being soft like a slug wasn't something to be happy about, especially if a woman was the one telling you. And that woman was French: her accent was unmistakable, and hadn't Felice himself named, after a Marisa who was none other than his mother, a "Jen'vieve," that is, a Geneviève? She, and not Marisa, was the first woman he had been with, and from the way she spoke, she must have been a prostitute. Had there been other women, later? I didn't have the heart to push that inquiry further, but if the slug had risen to become for him a symbol of all iniquity, there couldn't have been many others, and either way it wouldn't have changed the outcome. Poor Felice! In every slug that crept in the garden he saw his own shame, and so—*whack!*—he'd slice it in two . . . This still didn't explain why the smaller slugs, those brown and greenish ones, hadn't been infected with that terrible significance; or else it offered a perfect explanation: those slugs weren't linked to that nasty prostitute Geneviève's derision, and the reason was that, unlike the *rufus*, they hadn't grown fat on forty or so French corpses . . . A fact that forced me to retrace my steps and admit that Felice was effectively on par with Darwin and Mendel . . . Where in the world had I found that man? Ugly as a monster, awkward and pitiable as a veteran with a war-shattered mind, but capable of jaw-dropping flashes of ingenuity, and of appearing to you at night in the enchanting likeness of the lonesome rider Shane . . .

In any event, the cruel words of a French whore had weighed more heavily on his life than forty bodies stacked one on top of the other, more heavily than the image of a handsome dragoon . . . He should have developed a morbid hatred for the Russians and the Germans, and instead, due to a momentary physical shortcoming, he waged a war against the French . . . I couldn't even think about it—I was so angry that if I'd bumped into that Geneviève, I would have thrown a can of vitriol in that cursed floozy's face . . .

That same day, I interrogated my grandfather about his acquisition of the house. He answered my questions with the obliging phoniness one shows toward disturbed people when not wishing to upset them—but he did answer. For example, he told me that even though he knew French well, the negotiations with the Kropoffs had been carried out entirely in Italian, a fact that didn't surprise him given how long they had been in our country. I disagreed, pointing out that the Kropoffs never budged beyond their own front gate, to which he retorted that they could have learned Italian from books, a hypothesis that sounded grotesque to me. I asked if he had picked up any hint of dialect in their Italian; he thought about it for a moment, then responded in the affirmative: no Russian accent, no French accent, but a touch of Varesotto, yes . . . And this didn't surprise him? Not at all. In fact, he hadn't even noticed: he didn't become morbidly obsessed by these things, the way I did . . .

So that's what I was to him, a morbid little boy . . . I'd thought I was a Stevensonian adolescent, and now I discovered that, on the outside, one did not see my adventurous disquietude, one only saw a morbid pain in the neck . . . I stormed off angrily, but it only took a few paces for me to tell myself that, at the end of the day, morbidness really wasn't such a bad thing.

I would need a chemist to analyze the blood; a zoologist and a biologist to study those slugs; a historian to find out what a French platoon had been doing in the area; a psychologist who could clearly explain to me the difference between amnesia and repression; a psychiatrist to understand the significance of that rabbit who was first blinded and then, in a drawing, hanged; the ghost of a land registrar to piece together the history of our house prior to the Kropoffs; a geologist who could uncover where that hole under the barrel led . . .

The only thing I didn't need was a friend, because I had Felice; but Felice was getting worse and worse . . . I had noticed for a few weeks now that his spit was tinged with blood, though really his whole appearance was what conveyed a state of suffering. It was as if his structure were collapsing: increasingly hunched, dangling his arms like an orangutan, he gave the impression that at any given moment he might curl into himself like certain caterpillars. However, what worried me most was his mind: not only were his memory lapses becoming more frequent, but they tended to veer into an outright loss of consciousness, during which he stayed motionless, his eyes glued shut by a crust that thickened by the day. On those occasions, I had to shake him by his sleeve and shout his name; when he came to, he went back to what he had been in the middle of doing before he'd drifted off, seemingly unaware of the interruption.

In conditions such as these, trying to wrest something about his mother from the jealous hideaways of his mind was unthinkable. And so my assistance was limited to small-scale upkeep, especially since our previously established stopgaps no longer worked either. One morning, for example, I see the large hydrangea bush shaking oddly; I approach it cautiously, and *inside* the bush I see Felice, who's peeing. I walk away so as not to embarrass him, and when he reemerges I ask what he was doing in there. Pissing, he admits candidly, and even more candidly reveals that he wasn't able to find the toilet.

"But what about the arrows?"

"Th' who?"

"The black ones we put on the walls."

"Ah, 'em arrows."

"They point you to the toilet, don't you remember?"

"Ah, be'er t' be knowin' tha' afore."

On that occasion, I also saw his member for the first time. Maybe I had been conditioned to think so, but it truly did look like an *Arion rufus*! Identical, in fact! Only closer to purple than brownish red . . . It seemed that purple truly was the mark of that man. Even his scrotum, to the extent that it could be glimpsed through the thick clump of hydrangeas, presented a purplish hue . . . But most of all, it seemed an enormous scrotum: did he have orchitis, perhaps? I remembered this word because once, hearing my grandfather pronounce it, I'd thought it was something particular to orcs, and when he explained its meaning to me my disappointment was immeasurable. But now that I had been classified under the morbidly obsessed, how could I ask my grandfather to give Felice a medical examination because I had taken a peek at his distended scrotal sac?

In those final days of August, I went to his house to see him as often as I could. The disorder in his room had risen to unimaginable heights: dirty laundry and unwashed dishes lay all around, the contents of knocked-over cans remained spilled on the floor, and his mattress had slid off the wire frame and was covered in all kinds of filth; everywhere, blowflies and horseflies buzzed. I would try to tidy up a little each time, but by my next visit that spectacle had only grown worse. Now, once again, he no longer remembered his own name, but not a fleece flower in the whole world was up to the task. He had forgotten the name of Nasca, too, he didn't know if my grandmother was alive or dead, the words "lettuce" and "chicory" meant absolutely nothing to him, he gave mammoth quantities of food to the chickens and the rabbits and then didn't give a thought to them for days on end, so that those poor animals first stuffed themselves until they could burst, and then languished, scraping at the ground in search of crumbs . . . Only, he never forgot my grandfather, and I never stopped being his Michelín . . . Even when I showed him that hideous knickknack with the portraits of Kennedy, the pope, and Khrushchev, he asked me who the three of them were; though when he saw the paper with my name stuck on top of the glass, he exclaimed:

"But this 'ere, I know who 't be. Sure, 'tis yerself, me Michelín!"

I asked him about Kennedy: never heard of him.

"Of course you have, the one who was killed by Oswald."

Never heard that name.

"And the Great Rabbit?"

"Poor rabbit . . . poor cratur 'f a rabbit."

It was all I could get out of him. A moment later he was sprawled out on the naked frame, the iron net checkering his face; a belch, then he fell asleep. By now he didn't even go to the osteria, his brain cells independently producing an alcohol-like molecule in which to soak themselves.

That evening, I came back home in a rage and decided to force my grandfather to face the facts. When his rich friends called him over a tummy ache, he grabbed his medical briefcase and dashed off in his Morris Mini, whereas Felice could croak right in front of his eyes without him noticing. I burst into the room with the big fireplace, a prepared speech in my head, but I was immediately told to hush up: the miniseries with Romolo Valli, Alberto Lupo, and Mita Medici was just getting good, I'd need to come back later. As a result, I lost my momentum, and by the time the seemingly never-ending episode was finally over I had already gone to bed.

During the night I made up my mind: I'd get Carmen to talk. I didn't know how, but I'd get her to talk.

"Mrs. Carmen, Felice is slipping away."

She didn't say anything; then she stared me straight in the eyes.

"How much longer does he have?"

I explained to her that it wasn't a question of time, that he could still live for years, but that he was fading, as though his mind were rotting. Her eyes grew damp, and she turned away.

"We're the two people who love him the most in the whole town," I ventured.

"Which means . . .?"

"We shouldn't keep secrets from one another . . . secrets that have to do with him, I mean."

"What are you getting at?"

"Look, Mrs. Carmen, he's told me a few things. Some things he's explained, some I've figured out on my own, and so I've pieced together a general idea—"

"An idea of what?" She cut me off, testily. "An idea of what, at your age?"

"An idea of what his life must have been like." I stopped myself there for now. I would get to the rest later.

"So what do you want from me?"

"For you to tell me if I've guessed correctly or not, if things went how I think they did."

"And then?"

"And then, that's it. Only how things went."

"And then you'll go shouting it from the rooftops."

"No! I swear!"

"Listen here, I'm one to talk straight. I don't like your grandparents."

"I can understand that."

"They didn't send you here, did they?"

"The two of them? If my grandfather knew I was here, I'd never hear the end of it . . . He's not even happy that I've become friends with Felice."

"Yeah, I know that you're close friends." For the first time, she smiled. "If you knew how many times he's talked to me about you."

"Oh, really?"

"Yeah, his Michelín . . . He'd give his life for you, you know that?"

This time, I was the one to become teary-eyed. She invited me to sit down: I was in!

"So, let's hear what you know."

I told her everything I had pieced together, up to the deal with the samovar and no further. She stared at me while I spoke, utterly focused; every so often a half-smile crept onto her face, as though a detail in my story had touched her. She never interrupted me, and even after I had finished, she sat in silence for a little while.

"So?" I asked her shyly, no longer able to bear that silence.

"So, it seems to me you already know a lot. Good job, I have to give you credit."

"And the rest?"

"The rest what?"

"The pieces that are still missing from the story."

"For example?"

"Carmen, don't pretend you don't see it—it's obvious how many holes are left."

"And what if those holes are for the best?"

"Better to know everything at this point, don't you think? Does it seem right to you for me to be stranded halfway, left to wonder for the rest of my life?"

"No. It wouldn't be right because of your friendship—but only because of that."

She went to look for her cigarettes, lit one (the great partisan woman! Executioner of SS men!), crossed her legs, and started talking.

Going back to the late eighteen hundreds, the house had belonged to the count. No one knew his name, because everybody had always referred to him only as "the count." He lived alone and had no heirs, and tons of locals in Nasca worked directly or indirectly for him; she, too, had gone a few times as a little girl to help in the kitchen when he hosted big lunches. The full time servants, who lived in one of the outbuildings, were the Bianchini family, Alfredo and Marta, and their son Danilo. When the war broke out—the first one—Danilo left for the front, and two years later, when they called on the reserves, Alfredo left too. Neither of the two came back, because as fate would have it they both fell in battle just a couple of weeks apart, near Bainsizza, one to the west and the other to the east. And so only Marta was left to look after the garden and the animals, along with a woman or two who came to work by the hour.

"But what about Marisa?"

"Marisa had gone off a few years earlier, when she was still a young girl. She said that country life wasn't for her."

"What did she go off to do?"

"Oh, she got by."

"What does that mean?"

"Jesus, you really are little! She was on the game, you know what that means?"

"No."

"Lucky you only made it halfway . . . It means she worked as a prostitute."

"Ah."

She had a place right outside Luino, and usually worked the big road from Luino to Ponte Tresa or the lakeside road between Maccagno and the Swiss border. It seems she was very famous around those parts. Due to a purplish birthmark on her cheek that looked like wine dregs, everyone knew her as the Dreg Lass.

She led that life for at least three years, from 1906 to 1909, until a stranger got her pregnant. After giving birth to Felice, she couldn't find anyone to look after him for her, and she went back to Nasca so that her parents could take care of the child. To stop her from going back to walking the streets, they refused, leaving her with no choice but to stay there with them. The parish priest at the time, an extremely narrow-minded man, disregarded the church's official position on such matters and refused to baptize the baby, whose birth wasn't even registered. So it was that little Felice stayed simply Felice.

Then, like in the story of Cinderella, something out of a fairy tale happened. The old count saw her and fell in love. With the excuse that he had been without a personal maidservant for some time, he hired her to attend him directly, providing a room for her on the top floor. Now her parents regarded her with an augmented rancor: they scattered manure and cut the grass, she prepared fragrant teas; they cleaned the rabbit cages and picked fruit, she tucked in the count's sheets; they took care of her rug rat, she fluttered around the count. Things seemed settled, but in just a few years death swept everything away. In 1917, Alfredo and Danilo fell in battle, and at the end of the same year, pneumonia took Marta too. During the day, little Felice, who was almost eight, followed close behind his mother's skirt, but at night he slept on his own in the outbuilding: he had wanted it that way, and every attempt made by his mother to bring him to her bedroom only provoked terrible fits of hysteria.

In the winter of 1918 the count unexpectedly passed away as well. Upon opening his will, the notary announced to Marisa that the deceased had named her his sole heir, but that there were no assets other than the property itself. And so, to the great displeasure of the parish priest, the Dreg Lass became the house's sole owner; nonetheless, Felice still insisted on sleeping in his little room. But the Dreg Lass had syphilis, and she never had it treated: at the end of 1918, she died too.

The sole owner, at the age of nine, was now a little boy with no last name.

"Then the Kropoffs arrived . . ."

"Yeah, but not right away. They must have been lying low in Switzerland, because it was already 1919 when they showed up."

"So he was on his own for several months."

"Right, and even then he didn't want to abandon his room."

"But why did the Kropoffs come to Nasca, of all places?"

"Ah, that I couldn't tell you . . . Could be they had a network of informers, and they found out that there was a perfect house for them here, a house practically without an owner . . ."

"Do you know how much they paid him for it?"

"Quiet, I feel sick just thinking about it! Of course I know—the whole town knew."

"And no one did anything about it?"

"And what would you have had us do? The men had nearly all died in the war, we women didn't know anything about the law, the only one who could have said something was the priest, but you could count that out. The wretch must have seen it as the proper divine punishment . . ."

"And Felice?"

"Felice started working for them right from the get-go, first doing minor tasks, then they really had him slaving away."

"Which means he worked for them for a good twenty-six years . . ."

"Why twenty-six? Until 1955 makes thirty-six."

"Ah, right. But on a different note . . . is it true that Marisa talked to him about his father as if he was a hero?"

"And how do you know that? In any case, yes, it's true. I've never heard a woman talk so favorably about the man who ruined her. And you had to see the way he listened to her: he seemed to drink it all up with his eyes . . ."

"You don't know anything about that man, do you?"

"Nothing. Even Marisa couldn't have known who he was."

"Okay. Now we need to move on to the rest."

"What's the rest?"

"You know perfectly well."

"Listen, you're a sweet kid, but don't overdo it, eh?"

"I found the bodies."

"What bodies?"

"The bodies of the French and the bodies of the Germans who weren't Germans, the ones under the lawn and in the storage room."

She lit another cigarette without looking at me, then took a deep breath with her eyes closed.

"So you're in a hurry to grow up, is that it?"

"Quite the opposite, really. I'd rather never grow up."

"Well then, why don't you spend your time playing games, instead of sticking your nose where it doesn't belong?"

"But that was the game—I mean . . . I became wrapped up in it . . ."

"They're neat, skeletons, aren't they?"

I kept quiet, looking at her like an interrogator dead set on obtaining information.

"Oh, all right, you stubborn kid! All right!"

And so she confirmed what I had imagined. The Kropoffs were working as spies for the Nazis, and they had already caused several partisans to be captured. She and Giuàn, who were the heads of the local unit, had suspected them for some time, but never found any proof. Then, one evening, a messenger arrived out of breath from Laveno—a group of French sappers, sent to Castelletto Ticino to support the Second Division, had gotten lost and were heading in their direction. They absolutely needed to be intercepted and warned of the danger, because the SS had set up garrisons in both Caldé and Porto Valtravaglia, with Laveno constantly being patrolled too: the partisans manage to warn them, and so, before they arrive in Caldé, the French soldiers take the high road, the one to Rasate and Pessina; only instead of turning off to the south, they make another mistake and keep going straight toward Valtravaglia. When the partisans realize this, it's already too late: the French have entered Nasca from the south, and one of the first houses they come across is the Kropoffs' . . . I already knew the rest, because my reconstructed account was perfect. Powerless, the partisans watch the burial of all those bodies from the roof of a nearby house. The Russians, Carmen added, treated Felice just as harshly as the Oberführer must have treated them. What's more, while moving in to surround the house, the SS run into Piero, and they don't think twice before shooting him with a silencer. It's a step too far, someone's going to have to pay . . . They work out how to execute the three Russians, but they have to act prudently so that Felice won't end up caught in the middle. A few days pass, during which the Kropoffs must realize that something is afoot . . . Maybe Felice himself drops a few accidental hints, after his friends tell him that it won't be long before there'll be no one to boss him around anymore . . . The fact of the matter is that one evening, the Russians decide to split—the news of the war doesn't leave them with much hope anyway, they were going to have to leave sooner or later . . . They take out three German uniforms stored some time earlier for that very contingency, the woman cuts her hair, and . . . once again I know the rest— Carmen doesn't know how I've done it, I must be a demon . . .

"I don't actually know everything there is to know. What part Felice had in it, for instance. He told me that you killed one each, is that true?"

"Nonsense. He only managed to leave a scratch on the old man's neck, poor darling. Giuàn and I did everything."

"Another thing: why is he convinced that the French were killed by people from around here?"

"He never saw the Germans, he only saw the dead, the dead foreigners. Then he saw me and Giuàn kill another three foreigners, so he must have drawn his own conclusion: the dead all came from the outside, the killers all came from the inside . . ."

"But didn't you explain the situation to him?"

"You know how he is, don't you? I've never met anyone who was so easily influenced and so stubborn at the same time."

As the years passed, the killers lost their nationality, then their humanity too, becoming simply "they." But this was something I couldn't talk about with Carmen.

"And afterward, you kept the house for ten years . . ."

"You found that out too! Well, what were we supposed to do? He was only interested in his little room. Meanwhile, going to the land registry was dangerous, and so we had the idea of keeping those Russian bastards alive."

"You did the right thing. And who worked out the deal with my grandfather?"

"Giuàn, who was already living in Musadino and didn't have much time left, what with all the lead in him."

"You know that Felice remembers almost nothing of any of this?"

"I know. I should be happy about it. Instead, it saddens me."

"Carmen, you know that I'll never betray your trust."

"You'd better not!" And for the first time, she laughed.

"I still have a couple of questions."

"Let's hear them."

"Why does he say he grew up with the rabbits?"

"Huh . . . I think it's because when he was little, he used to always go into where they kept the rabbits, first following his grandmother, then of his own accord, when it was just him and his mother. He'd sometimes spend half the day in there, talking to the rabbits . . ."

"Who is the Great Rabbit?"

"Never heard of it."

"Never heard of a blinded and hanged rabbit?"

"Never."

"In our cellar there are lots of bottles that are half-filled with something that looks like hardened must, but is actually blood. Do you know anything about those?"

"No."

"But in '45 they were already there, right?"

"Seems to me they were. Any other questions?"

"No . . . Actually, yes: what was this municipality called before it became Castelveccana?"

"Castelvaltravaglia."

Really, I would have liked to ask her more, above all how many Germans and how many Fascists she had killed, and where, and how, and who her surviving comrades were, and where they lived . . . But the deal was that we shouldn't have secrets concerning Felice, and these were questions that didn't concern him.

But the time for my ruminations had not yet come to an end. Marisa Bianchini had died of syphilis at the age of twenty-seven. If she already had that disease when her son was born, she could have passed it on to him, and this, rather than a malady on his father's side, could have been the initial cause of his mnemonic woes. I asked my grandfather if syphilis was hereditary, and he said it was, even if the symptoms often changed from one generation to the next; I asked him if it could damage a person's memory, and he replied that it damaged the entire nervous system, meaning that one couldn't exclude the possibility of syphilis causing memory problems in certain individuals.

"Problems"! That we were talking about Felice hadn't even crossed his mind. He had probably chalked my questions up to my "morbidness" . . .

But why had Felice been so categorical in attributing his amnesia to a paternal inheritance? It certainly couldn't have been his mother—forever singing the dragoon's praises—who had planted that idea in his head . . . Could it have been merely an instance of linguistic imprecision, whereby he did mean to refer to a father, but to his mother's father, that is, Alfredo? But there was no evidence that pointed to him, otherwise Carmen would have mentioned it . . .

And the presumed must? The *rufus* slugs had grown big feasting on the French, but what if someone had already been seeking to create a race of carnivorous slugs? The hypothesis came to me straight from all the horror films I had seen, but the idea of a super-race flung me right back into Nazi territory, immediately turning my adventure grim . . . It turned grim, but it continued: I pictured old Kropoff, under orders from Berlin, watering the lettuce with blood and compiling his findings each month (but why? What would those big Nazi slugs be used for?) . . . Then the experiment expanded to include other animal species, for example rabbits: one of which is fed a special blood-based diet, and, lo and behold, it grows faster than the rest, faster and bigger and, naturally, meaner . . . the Great Rabbit! Mystery solved . . . Young Felice looks upon it with a mix of admiration and horror, until something goes wrong in the experiment and the monster has to be killed . . . or, rather, the experiment goes perfectly, and the beast has to be sent to Berlin as proof, and so it's killed and put in a sealed case where no one can go snooping around . . . And what if, instead of genetics, it had to do with the occult? The high-ranking Nazis were all obsessed with the occult, a fact that was even noted in my school textbook . . . Maybe, then, that blood was intended for a harrowing black ritual . . . In that case, "Great Rabbit" could have been the name of a high priest . . . Or, speaking of priests, what if Felice had misunderstood, and the Nazis had spoken of plans to take out an influential rabbi? And if the Nazis actually had nothing to do with it? If the mad experimenter was the count? If he was a Freemason? Whenever my mania took hold of me like this, I knew I could go on multi-plying hypotheses indefinitely, spinning in a vertigo in which every addition was a subtraction . . .

What I needed was new elements, but Felice was by now incapable of supplying me with them . . . or was he? And if, on the contrary, his very psychasthenia had freed secrets that had been kept jealously hidden until now? I went to see him after lunch: as usual, he was lying on the metal bed frame, while everything around him was even messier and dirtier than the last time. He seemed to be sleeping, but as soon as I made the slightest noise, he turned toward me.

"Michelín, 's'ye there?"

"Yes."

"Can't be seein' ye no . . . can't be op'nin' me eyes."

Bloated and purplish, his eyelids were literally glued together by a now crystallized secretion that imprisoned his lashes like blades of grass in amber. With a soaked rag, I washed them for him, but to remove those crystals I had to go back to our house to get tweezers. He endured the operation without emitting so much as a breath, until he opened his eyes and seemed shocked to have so much in view.

"'M after fin'in' me eyes, Michelín, me eyes!"

Following first his grandmother, then his mother, whenever he came over to our house he went into the rabbit hutch . . .

"For how long have you had this problem with your eyes?"

"Ah, long time, so, long time . . . since I were a wee lad, always blin' as a ba', like . . ."

He considered the rabbits his brothers . . . his mother pro-tected him with fairy tales . . . He was the Great Rabbit! The loss of the rabbit's eyes was a detail that he must have added years later, when his chronic pinkeye worsened . . . I looked at where he had drawn the hanged rabbit, but now there was nothing there, only the shadow left by a hand rubbing against the wardrobe door.

"Felice, you were the Great Rabbit."

"Eh? I dunno, dunno 't'all . . . I dun' . . . Eh? Rabbiss? I dunno . . ."

He was exhausted, I couldn't torture him like that. I gave him a kiss on the forehead and left.

As soon I set foot inside our house, I overheard a few bits of conversation between my grandfather and grandmother—or rather, as always, of incontestable statements made by my grandfather and directed at my grandmother. The topic was none other than the idea of firing Felice due to his manifest inability to work.

Without even thinking, I burst into the room and assailed them with my indignation—he a doctor, no less, with his stinking Hippocratic oath . . . I don't remember what I said, I only know that they looked at me as though I was in the throes of a hysterical fit, and maybe I was . . . I ended by saying that if they fired him they would never see me again. Then, to calm down, I took my bicycle and pedaled for an hour on the hills.

When I came back, it was already past dinnertime, and my grandparents were sitting glued to the television, under the spell of Renzo Palmer and Virna Lisi.

I found Renzo Palmer likable, with that chubby face and that crisp dubber's voice of his . . . But a miniseries adaptation is a miniseries adaptation; in other words, pure evil . . . Maybe evil was not as enchanting as I'd always wanted it to be, maybe it didn't consist of demons and monsters . . . And even adventure, which I could conceptualize only in the ways established by Stevenson, by Melville, and by the other greats who had taken me by the hand, even adventure had perhaps ended with them, and all that remained of it now was a shabby caricature on "children's television," in certain horrible shows like *The Children of Father Tobia*, which immediately prompted me to feel unwell from the first appearance of Silvano Tranquilli's face . . .

That night, I thought a great deal about the count. If I opened a file on him too, where would it take me? How many years of my life would I spend, perhaps only to arrive at the conclusion that he was an individual lacking in any interest whatsoever? He had laid eyes on that fallen woman and had taken her for himself—did he know she was a prostitute? I would've bet he did; in numerous books, I had encountered stories of men who took pleasure in redeeming women like her, the so-called dregs of society . . . And to think, at his age—not that I knew anything about these things . . . but if Felice, in the prime of his youth, had been made fun of by that French prostitute, then the old count couldn't have had much hope of doing better . . . The Dreg Lass, however, would have steered clear of deriding him, for she had a child to look after and a family from which she wanted to free herself . . . There wasn't a whole lot of adventure in this, as a matter of fact; I much preferred the part with the skeletons . . .

The memory of Geneviève was like a synapse: but of course! How had I not thought of it before! Wasn't syphilis also called the "French disease"? The Dreg Lass surely wouldn't have mentioned this around her son—but her snakes of parents? Probably Marta, not caring if the child overheard . . . or maybe precisely so that he would hear . . . Consequently, he's impelled to think of his father: his malady comes from the dragoon, it comes from the French, but especially—so he'll think years later— from the ones who are closest to his home and underneath our lawn, and it comes from the slugs who are also, in their own way, the descendants of those Frenchmen . . . The slugs as plague spreaders—that was the first thing to come to my mind, years later, when I read about Settala and Ripamonti in *The Betrothed* . . . In that moment, however, recalling my grandfather's explanations, I thought of the slugs as giant spirochetes . . .

If his grandparents had done everything in their power to turn that poor child against his mother, they would have had no qualms about painting an unfavorable picture of her past life. But was this enough for that child, as he grew up, to erase the memory of that mother, progressing to a radical destruction of anything that could reevoke her? Who knows, maybe in that lodging of theirs on the outskirts of Luino, the little one had witnessed his mother's relations with clients on multiple occasions . . . In any event, the complete purge enacted in his room corresponded to an act of mental repression and erasure, and the bigger that void became, the more he needed to fill it with an alternative, and what alternative could have lent itself to that purpose if not the enchanting dragoon? Thus, the character from a fairy tale became a legend he had to find again—that is, another kind of void . . .

I must have fallen asleep then and started to dream, because the count was identical to Bela Lugosi, which explained only too well the blood stored in the bottles . . . Having grown vulgar in the Varesotto, the noble Transylvanian must have switched from the blood of beautiful virgins to that of pigs and rabbits, which apparently worked just as well . . . Then he looked at me, laughing, his mouth completely smeared with blood, and said: "But do you really believe it?" Whereupon he ripped off his mask in the manner of Diabolik, and he was the actor Arnoldo Foà. Another laugh, and he took off that mask too: now he was Giampiero Albertini, who, his mask removed, turned out to be Paolo Ferrari—then, mask after mask, he became Massimo Serato, Andrea Giordana, Sergio Fantoni, Gino Cervi, Aroldo Tieri, Ugo Pagliai, and each time I was convinced that this was the real one, the last one: instead, like the skin of an onion, the masks kept peeling off, one after the other, and Nino Castelnuovo made way for Alberto Lionello, who made way for Raf Vallone, who became Gabriele Ferzetti, but only to turn into Romolo Valli—Valli then became Claudio Gora, whose features covered those of Adalberto Maria Merli, who was immediately replaced by Umberto Orsini, though Orsini was none other than Luigi Vannucchi, who in reality was Glauco Mauri, underneath whose countenance lay hidden the visage of Orso Maria Guerrini, who wanted nothing more than to show me how quickly he could transform into Riccardo Cucciolla . . . "Stop! Stop!" I screamed. "Tell me who you are!" And Cucciolla, in whose shifting face simultaneously flitted all the other faces, said (although at this point he was already much more Foà than Cucciolla, with a lot of Merli and a lot of Orsini, and the voice of Paolo Stoppa): "Who am I? Why, I am the king of the miniseries! And I want to live forever, so that the multitudes of miniseries will never end! And for this I need blood, lots and lots of blood!" And he pointed to the bottles, in which the blood was still liquid and red, blood that rose to the brim; then he pointed to a dark corner of the cellar, where, straining my eyes, I could make out the Dreg Lass, who was covered only by a scanty white nightgown and shackled to the wall, her skin even whiter than her nightgown, while numerous slugs had attached themselves to her legs and arms like bloodsucking leeches, some more slender, others already swollen like ticks . . . Then the count, with the youthful bravado of Andrea Giordana and Giuseppe Pambieri, though also with the gravity of Gino Cervi and Tino Buazzelli, walked over to her and ripped off the most swollen slugs, and, raising them over an empty bottle into which a funnel had been stuck, squeezed them like grapes: screeching horribly, the mollusks issued copious amounts of blood which sparkled as it flowed into the bottle, whereupon—emptied remains—they were tossed into a bin.

I woke in the grip of a distress that would last the whole day. How many times had Marisa Bianchini died? At least five: when she went on the road to Ponte Tresa; when she was shunned by the parish priest and treated as plague-ridden by her family; every time the count's slugs sucked her blood; when she died a biological death; and when she was forgotten by her son. It was only a dream, but in me it became true—it was like a musical score, and I the instrument playing it . . . A horrific dream, but with a hidden consolation: that blood was syphilitic, and in drinking it, the king of the miniseries hastened his own end . . .

It was three in the morning. I went downstairs to the kitchen to heat up some milk, and the oilcloth on the table was covered in red slugs. They were motionless, arranged in concentric circles as though for an occult ritual.

In the middle of the smallest circle were two eyeballs staring up at the ceiling.

At the head of the table, wrapped in an old purplish quilt, sat Felice, his eyelids completely welded shut. In his hand he held a glass full of blood.

"You were the one who did this," he said. "You used to cut the throats of rabbits and hold them upside down until all the blood had dripped into the bottle."

"But when?"

"A long time ago. You can't remember."

"I don't know what you're talking about . . ."

"Well, not you exactly . . . Do you remember when I told you about the Michelino from before? The one who is sleeping now?"

Did I remember!

"That's right, it was him, and I had to help him."

"Felice, I'm going to take you back home now and put you to bed."

"You don't understand: I'm the one who has to put you to sleep. He spoke to me and he told me that it's time to be woken up."

"It's a dream, tell me it's a dream."

"That you're able to ask that question should make you see that it's no dream. I'm sorry, Michelino, I loved you a lot, truly, and I know that you loved me too. But he is stronger."

"What does that mean, stronger?"

"It means older, more ancient, and age is everything in this house."

"In this house . . ."

"In this house. A house in Castelvaltravaglia—forget about Castelveccana."

"What is going to happen now?"

"Nothing, you'll warm your milk and then we'll pour this glass into it. Then you'll go to sleep and . . . that's all, nothing more will happen."

"But tomorrow morning, he'll be the one to wake up, won't he?"

"The slugs are disoriented, for too long now they've been in need of a guide. Try to understand . . ."

"You won't cut them in half anymore with the spade, then?"

"Well, it seems I'll have to stop . . . I let off some steam while you were here, but now it will be necessary to toe the line."

"And your memory?"

"He'll take care of that, putting into it whatever is required. That's what he has always done. Just as he has with language. If he wishes, he can make me speak all the languages of the world."

"And are you happy?"

"I cannot choose, no one has ever been able to choose. Not even you. He let you have a little fun, but now: time's up."

They were *he*; he was who I had been, and soon I would be him again.

"And the verdigris?"

"What about the verdigris?"

"Nothing. Just thought I'd ask."

TRANSLATOR'S NOTE

When it comes to the pleasures of reading, there is no such thing as growing up. Or at least certain works of literature make it tempting to think so—as if there were always the same young reader buried inside us, one who comes back to life each time we lose ourselves in the beauty and mystery of a good book. For me, Michele Mari's *Verdigris* is one such book. When I read it for the first time, I relived a mix of excitement and suspense, of elation and tension and horror that I thought had ended with the books and stories of my childhood. Having found the novel so enjoyable and gripping, and its world so thoroughly immersive, I wanted to recreate that experience and that world as fully as possible for anglophone readers. What I mean, essentially, is that I wanted this translation to *live* as a book in English, and remain, like Mari's original—for which I'll use the Italian title of *Verderame* going forward—a unique celebration of language and an utterly absorbing mystery. Conversely, what I did not want it to be was a series of humorless footnotes, of arrows pointing to the significance of Italian words and puns, while asking readers to imagine for themselves linguistic dynamics that weren't recreated by the translation itself. It's therefore worth detailing how I approached the two central linguistic elements that pull the reader into this rabbit hole of a novel, and which can be divided into the two categories of wordplay, or word association, and of dialect.

Far from being ornamental, wordplay serves a very specific function in *Verdigris*. When thirteen-year-old Michelino—who spends every summer at his grandparents' house in the town of Nasca, near Lake Maggiore—learns that their gardener and general factotum Felice is losing his memory, he tries to create a mnemonic system to help piece his fractured world back together. As Felice forgets more and more words, Michelino supplies a new alphabet composed of images and objects that spark an immediate association through sound, thereby recalling the name of the forgotten thing. The point of most of the wordplay is, therefore, its immediacy. For this reason, the associations I have used in English are intended to feel just as direct; otherwise, they would serve very little use to Felice and would contradict their stated purpose. This has required a few minor shifts in the dialogue between the two characters, a couple of altered anecdotes, but no significant changes to the story itself. In making these adjustments (all of which have received Michele Mari's complete approval) I have considered it essential that they fit naturally in the context of the novel and in what could be called the broader Mari universe. For example, while the name of Nasca is originally evoked by the baby from a nativity scene and the word *nascita*, or "birth," in the translation it is recalled by the word "NASCAR" written on one of Michelino's Mercury toy cars, a childhood obsession that will already be familiar to readers of Mari's story collection *You, Bleeding Childhood* (And Other Stories, 2023). As opposed to the majority of these individual mnemonic associations, the most complicated instance of wordplay, which even involves an unforgettable anagram, proves to be a key piece in the mystery animating the novel. Accordingly, the English version of this multilayered puzzle does not entail any significant break from Mari's original, but instead creates an extremely faithful parallel.

The novel's linguistic complexities are heightened by the fact that the character Felice speaks only in dialect. First of all, it should be noted that dialects in Italy are not derivations from standard Italian, which has its foundation in Florentine; most Northern Italian dialects are generally classified in a different group of Romance languages, often referred to as Gallo-Italic. This means that in *Verderame* Michelino and Felice essentially speak to each other in two distinct languages. Felice's dialogue thus presents considerable difficulties for Italian readers who are unfamiliar with Gallo-Italic dialects—in other words, the majority of Italian readers today, with even regional use of these dialects in the north declining precipitously with every new generation—but quite often Michelino's responses lend an interpretive hand. Surprisingly, the book's effective multilingualism can actually help the reader follow the story: every line of dialogue, every word in fact, makes immediately plain which of the two characters is speaking, and this is a feature that I have tried to preserve. Mari has long been hailed as one of Italy's most linguistically gifted authors, capable of inventing new languages—including those of supernatural creatures and monsters—and of beautifully recreating older literary styles and forms. To put it plainly, there is no world in which this author would have written such a dialogue-heavy book with both speakers communicating in everyday Italian. The implication for the translation is quite simple: to lose the book's sense of linguistic inventiveness and diversity, by having both characters speak the same standard form of English, would have meant losing the book.

While the presence of dialect in general can complicate the task of a translator, Felice's speech in *Verderame* is extremely particular. Felice comes from a small town in the Varesotto, an area comprising Varese and its hinterland in the northwesternmost part of Italy's Lombardy region. Mari, a Milanese author who did not grow up speaking a dialect himself, relied heavily on literary texts to create Felice's speech, but these sources were principally Milanese. This is partly because Milanese, in comparison to the Varesotto dialect, has an especially rich poetic history, and Mari drew on a range of poets spanning from the eighteenth to the twentieth centuries. With a Milanese foundation, Felice's speech in the novel is rounded out with elements of Varesotto and other Lombard and Northern Italian dialects, resulting in a willful pastiche. It should also be noted that although Milan and the Varesotto are both in Lombardy, Italian dialects do vary considerably even within the same region. So, while it is realistic that a rural character like Felice would speak in dialect in the 1960s, his speech itself seems to present a break from reality. Mari has always maintained that his novel, despite taking direct inspiration from real-life figures and events, is a gothic fantasy, and Felice's geographically imprecise language can be considered a part of this fantasy, just as certain erudite qualities of young Michelino's dialogue invite readers to suspend their disbelief. The fact that these two characters continuously understand each other, without any real hiccups, subtly intensifies the novel's surreal quality from its opening pages. In short, no Italian reader would fully recognize their own language in Felice's, and many readers would encounter it as something inherently foreign.

Though the situation concerning dialects in English is quite different, I have sought to maintain these integral parts of Mari's novel, with Felice's and Michelino's speech remaining as distinct from one another as possible, and with Felice communicating in a manner that is all his own, a personal language that does not closely adhere to any reader's spoken reality, and which instead sets this lonely character further apart from the other figures in the book, all of whom speak standard Italian in the original. At the same time, actual dialectal and vernacular traits do not exist in a vacuum or untied from specific locations and communities, and the speech of the anglophone Felice largely finds inspiration in different modes of British and, even more so, Irish speech—though the result is, again, a knowingly unfaithful and rather unbelievable amalgam. While it would be inherently absurd to claim that any location in the Anglosphere is equivalent to the Varesotto (and it's perhaps no less arbitrary or absurd to claim that Italian characters should speak a supposedly neutral mid-Atlantic English, which is often desired in translations), there are various reasons why Felice seems at home in an Irish-influenced voice, reasons that go beyond more superficial associations in the international popular imagination, such as with rural settings. The novel's protagonist, Michelino, sees the world through a literary lens, and many of Felice's supernatural beliefs will feel familiar to readers of Irish literature and folklore. His conviction that the dead go on talking underground, for instance, is reminiscent of the most famous Irish-language novel ever written, Máirtín Ó Cadhain's *Cré na Cille*, just as his warning that the *real* versions of people have been replaced by copies mirrors the folklore of fairies and changelings.

But more than anything, I wrote Felice's speech the way I *heard* Felice's speech, in all its eccentricities and contradictions, from the moment I imagined the character in English. In placing myself in the shoes of the novel's young protagonist, I realize I have essentially done to the anglophone Felice what Mari and Michelino together did to the original character. Felice's language in *Verderame* is a mix of childhood associations and of pure literature: pieces of dialect learned in Nasca, where Mari spent his childhood summers, and in his hometown of Milan, melded with the formal dialect of poetic traditions, with the language of literary texts. Irish speech patterns were constantly present in my childhood and among my immediate family before

I ever lived in the country, but—and perhaps more importantly—Hiberno-English has found much of its most persistent literary expression in written forms that echo but do not wholly match people's actual speech, such as the poetic and dramatic vernaculars of the Irish Literary Revival in the early twentieth century, or the dialogue in the Irish gothic, Romantic, and folkloric texts that came before it.

For the most part, Felice's speech in the translation is not written to match any specific accent phonetically. At times I have used alternate spellings or variants, such as "divil" for "devil," or "ye" for "you," the pronunciation of which is closer to "yeh" or "yuh" than to "yee." Many of these variants—which continue to be used particularly in Ireland, and in some cases in Scotland—actually connect back to older English spellings and pronunciations, and should not be misinterpreted as deviations from today's standard English. For the most part, the spelling differences in Felice's speech, which I've used as a further means of distinction, are instead due to his many elisions and truncated words: to the extent that his written speech is phonetic, it is generally so in highlighting what sounds he does *not* produce. Felice, as we learn from the very first pages, is losing his memory, forgetting even the most essential words, and these skipped letters and sounds are also intended to give the more immediate impression that his speech is coming apart at the seams, disintegrating, or "losing pieces of itself," to quote the narrator.

This is just one way in which Felice's dialect, rather than being lost or hidden, is meant to play an active role in the translation. The use of dialect and vernacular—once incredibly common in the dialogue of anglophone literature, and an inextricable part of many of its most famous characters—has gradually become less widespread, and the reader of *Verdigris* might instinctively feel that Felice's speech is a feature that "now truly belong[s] to literature, and to an old literature at that," to repurpose the words of Michelino once again. The very presence of this willfully exaggerated dialect sends an implicit message that we are in a literary world, a world imbued with gothic horror and fairy tales, with mystery and fantasy, with nineteenth-century adventure novels, detective stories, and bildungsromans. Michelino, in fact, knowingly projects the books he has absorbed onto his companion, and Mari's decision to have Felice speak in a dialect, one that isn't shared by the book's narrator or protagonist, is a nod to older literary conventions, and especially to the use of vernacular in gothic and adventure fiction written in English. Again, this is not to say literature exclusively from England—the two unnamed works of gothic fiction that loom the largest, that of the vampire and that of the monstrous double, were written by authors from Ireland and Scotland: Bram Stoker and Robert Louis Stevenson. In terms of the latter, Michelino is steeped not only in his *Strange Case of Dr. Jekyll and Mr. Hyde*, and an important influence in blurring Felice's anglophone speech—and in making it all the more unique and unplaceable—has been the vernacular speech of Stevenson's adventure novels, especially the one Michelino loves the most, *Treasure Island*. Felice, after all, is never shown having a conversation with any characters besides this thirteen-year-old boy, and we might wonder if other people would hear the same speech at all, or if what Michelino hears is to a certain extent another literary projection. Finally, if any of these influences on Felice's anglophone speech should seem tenuous or arbitrary, one should consider that the question of arbitrariness—as well as that of projection and ventriloquism—is addressed directly in the novel's final pages, in one of the most memorable scenes in the history of Italian horror.

The real-life Felice, as Mari has revealed to me, actually did speak in a manner that was entirely unique, in his own idiolect, and this is also the case in the translation. His mode of communication is just one of the many elements that definitively place this character in the category of the *other*; or to put it in Michelino's supernatural terms: "The charm of that whole story, moreover, was bound up in the fact that it concerned another, not to mention those quintessential *others* who are monsters." Though the real Felice apparently spoke very little, and quite unintelligibly, in literature Michelino and Felice can communicate endlessly, carrying out all the imagined conversations that never took place in real life, with Michelino assuming the all-important role of Felice whisperer. Our protagonist acts as a bridge between the outside world and the wholly singular language of his companion, a figure who is both protective monster and fragile friend, a product of literature and a resurrected piece of the author's past.

BRIAN ROBERT MOORE
New York, March 2023

THIS BOOK WAS MADE POSSIBLE
THANKS TO THE SUPPORT OF

Aaron McEnery
Aaron Schneider
Abigail Walton
Adam Lenson
Ajay Sharma
Al Ullman
Alasdair Cross
Alastair
  Gillespie
Albert Puente
Alex Pearce
Alex Pheby
Alex Ramsey
Alexandra
  Stewart
Alexandra
  Tammaro
Alexandra Webb
Ali Riley
Ali Smith
Ali Usman
Alice Clarke
Alice Wilkinson
Alison Hardy
Aliya Rashid
Alyssa Rinaldi
Alyssa Tauber
Amado Floresca
Amaia Gabantxo
Amanda
Amanda Astley
Amanda Dalton
Amber Da
Amelia Dowe
Amitav Hajra
Amos
  Hintermann
Amy Hatch

Amy Lloyd
Amy Sousa
Amy Tabb
Ana Novak
Andra Dusu
Andrea Barlien
Andrea Larsen
Andrea
  Oyarzabal
  Koppes
Andreas
  Zbinden
Andrew Kerr-
  Jarrett
Andrew
  Marston
Andrew Martino
Andrew
  McCallum
Andrew Place
Andrew Place
Andrew Rego
Andrew Wright
Andrzej
  Walzchojnacki
Andy Marshall
Angelina Izzo
Angus Walker
Ann Morgan
Ann Rees
Anna-Maria
  Aurich
Anna French
Anna Gibson
Anna
  Hawthorne
Anna Holmes
Anna Kornilova

Anna Milsom
Anna Zaranko
Anne Edyvean
Anne
  Germanacos
Anne Kangley
Anne-Marie
  Renshaw
Anne Willborn
Annette Volger
Anonymous
Anthony Cotton
Anthony
  Fortenberry
Anthony Quinn
Antonia Saske
Antony Pearce
April Hernandez
Archie Davies
Aron Trauring
Asako Serizawa
Ashleigh Sutton
Audrey Holmes
Audrey Mash
Audrey Small
Barbara Mellor
Barbara Spicer
Barry John
  Fletcher
Barry Norton
Becky
  Cherriman
Becky
  Matthewson
Ben Buchwald
Ben Schofield
Ben Thornton
Ben Walter

Benjamin Judge
Benjamin Pester
Beth Heim de
  Bera
Betty Roberts
Beverley Thomas
Bianca Winter
Bill Fletcher
Billy-Ray
  Belcourt
Bjørnar
  Djupevik
  Hagen
Blazej Jedras
Brandon Clar
Brenda Wrobel
Brendan Dunne
Briallen Hopper
Brian Anderson
Brian Byrne
Brian Isabelle
Brian Smith
Briana Sprague
Bridget Prentice
Briony Hey
Brittany Redgate
Brooks Williams
Buck Johnston
  & Camp
  Bosworth
Burkhard
  Fehsenfeld
Buzz Poole
Caitlin Halpern
Cam Scott
Cameron Adams
Camilla
  Imperiali

Douglas Smoot
Dugald Mackie
Duncan
  Chambers
Duncan Clubb
Duncan
  Macgregor
Dustin Chase-
  Woods
Dyanne Prinsen
Earl James
Ebba
  Tornérhielm
Ed Smith
Edward
  Champion
Ekaterina
  Beliakova
Elaine Rodrigues
Eleanor Maier
Eleanor
  Updegraff
Elif Aganoglu
Elina Zicmane
Elizabeth
  Atkinson
Elizabeth
  Balmain
Elizabeth
  Braswell
Elizabeth
  Coombes
Elizabeth Draper
Elizabeth Franz
Elizabeth Guss
Elizabeth Leach
Elizabeth Rice
Elizabeth Seals
Elizabeth
  Sieminski
Ella Sabiduria
Ellen Agnew

Ellen
  Beardsworth
Emiliano Gomez
Emily Gladhart
Emma
  Barraclough
Emma Bielecki
Emma Louise
  Grove
Emma Morgan
Emma Post
Eric Anderson
Erin Cameron
  Allen
Erin Feeley
Ethan White
Evelyn Reis
Ewan Tant
Fay Barrett
Felicity Le
  Quesne
Felix Valdivieso
Finbarr
  Farragher
Fiona Liddle
Fiona Mozley
Fiona Wilson
Forrest Pelsue
Fran Sanderson
Frances Dinger
Frances Harvey
Francesca
  Brooks
Francesca
  Rhydderch
Frank Pearson
Frank Rodrigues
Frank van
  Orsouw
Gala Copley
Gavin Aitchison
Gawain Espley

Gemma Bird
Gemma Hopkins
Geoff Thrower
Geoffrey Cohen
Geoffrey Urland
George Stanbury
George
  Wilkinson
Georgia
  Shomidie
Georgina
  Hildick-Smith
Georgina
  Norton
Gerry Craddock
Gill Boag-
  Munroe
Gillian Grant
Gillian Spencer
Gillian Stern
Gina Filo
Gina Heathcote
Glen Bornais
Glenn Russell
Gloria Gunn
Gordon
  Cameron
Gosia Pennar
Grace Payne
Graham
  Blenkinsop
Graham R Foster
Grant Ray-
  Howett
Hadil Balzan
Halina
  Schiffman-
  Shilo
Hannah Freeman
Hannah Rapley
Hannah
  Vidmark

Hannah Jane
  Lownsbrough
Hans Lazda
Harriet Stiles
Haydon
  Spenceley
Heidi Gilhooly
Helen Alexander
Henrike
  Laehnemann
Holly Down
Howard
  Robinson
Hyoung-Won
  Park
Iain Forsyth
Ian Betteridge
Ian McMillan
Ian Mond
Ida Grochowska
Imogen Clarke
Ines Alfano
Inga Gaile
Irene Mansfield
Irina Tzanova
Isabella Garment
Isabella
  Weibrecht
J Drew Hancock-
  Teed
JE Crispin
Jack Brown
Jacob Musser
Jacqueline
  Lademann
Jacquelynn
  Williams
Jake Baldwinson
Jake Newby
James Avery
James Beck
James Crossley

James Cubbon
James Higgs
James Kinsley
James Leonard
James Portlock
James Richards
James Ruland
James
  Scudamore
Jamie Mollart
Jan Hicks
Jane Bryce
Jane Dolman
Jane Leuchter
Jane Roberts
Jane Roberts
Jane Woollard
Janet Digby
Janis Carpenter
Janna Eastwood
Jasmine Gideon
Jason Bell
Jason Montano
Jason Sim
Jason
  Timermanis
Jeanne Guyon
Jeff Collins
Jeff Fesperman
Jen Hardwicke
Jenifer Logie
Jennifer Fain
Jennifer Fosket
Jennifer Mills
Jennifer Watts
Jennifer
  Yanoschak
Jenny Huth
Jenny McNally
Jeremy Koenig
Jeremy Morton
Jeremy Sabol

Jerome Mersky
Jerry Simcock
Jess Wood
Jesse Coleman
Jessica Gately
Jessica Laine
Jessica Queree
Jessica Weetch
Jethro Soutar
Jill Harrison
Joanna Luloff
Joanna
  Trachtenberg
Joao Pedro
  Bragatti
  Winckler
JoDee Brandon
Jodie Adams
Joe Huggins
Joel Swerdlow
Johannes
  Holmqvist
Johannes
  Menzel
John Berube
John Bogg
John Carnahan
John Conway
John Gent
John Hodgson
John Kelly
John Miller
John Purser
John Reid
John Shadduck
John Shaw
John Steigerwald
John Walsh
John Whiteside
John Winkelman
Jolene Smith
Jon Riches

Jonathan Blaney
Jonathan Harris
Jonathan Huston
Jonathan
  Paterson
Joni Chan
Jonny
  Kiehlmann
Jordana Carlin
Joseph Camilleri
Joseph
  Darlington
Joseph Thomas
Josephine
  Glöckner
Josh Glitz
Josh Sumner
Joshua Briggs
Joshua Davis
Joy Paul
Judith Gruet-
  Kaye
Julia Foden
Julia Von Dem
  Knesebeck
Julie Atherton
Julie Greenwalt
Juliet Swann
Junius Hoffman
Jupiter Jones
Juraj Janik
Justine
  Sherwood
KL Ee
Kaarina Hollo
Kaja R Anker-
  Rasch
Kalina Rose
Kamaryn Norris
Karen Gilbert
Karen Mahinski
Karin Mckercher

Karl Kleinknecht
  & Monika
  Motylinska
Katarzyna
  Bartoszynska
Kate Beswick
Kate Carlton-
  Reditt
Kate Rizzo
Katharine
  Robbins
Kathrin Zander
Kathryn Burruss
Kathryn
  Edwards
Kathryn
  Williams
Katie Brown
Katie Cooke
Katie Freeman
Katie Grant
Katy Robinson
Kavitha Buggana
Kay
  Cunningham
Keith Walker
Kelly Hydrick
Kelsey Grashoff
Kenneth Blythe
Kenneth
  Peabody
Kent McKernan
Kerry Broderick
Kerry Parke
Kieran Rollin
Kieron James
Kris Ann Trimis
Kristen
  Tcherneshoff
Kristen Tracey
Kristy
  Richardson

Krystale Tremblay-Moll
Krystine Phelps
Kurt Navratil
Kyle Pienaar
Kyra Wilder
Lacy Wolfe
Lana Selby
Laura Ling
Laura Murphy
Laura Pugh
Laura Rangeley
Lauren Pout
Lauren Trestler
Laurence Laluyaux
Leah Binns
Lee Harbour
Leona Iosifidou
Liliana Lobato
Lilie Weaver
Lily Blacksell
Linda Jones
Linda Milam
Linda Whittle
Lindsay Attree
Lindsay Brammer
Lindsey Ford
Lindsey Harbour
Lisa Leahigh
Lisa Simpson
Liz Clifford
Liz Ketch
Liz Ladd
Lorna Bleach
Louise Evans
Louise Greenberg
Louise Jolliffe
Lucinda Smith
Lucy Moffatt

Luise von Flotow
Luiz Cesar Peres
Luke Murphy
Lydia Syson
Lynda Graham
Lyndia Thomas
Lynn Fung
Lynn Grant
Lynn Martin
Madalyn Marcus
Madden Aleia
Maeve Lambe
Maggie Humm
Malgorzata Rokicka
Mandy Wight
Marco Medjimorec
Mari-Liis Calloway
Maria Lomunno
Maria Losada
Marie Cloutier
Marijana Rimac
Marina Castledine
Marion Pennicuik
Marja S Laaksonen
Mark Reynolds
Mark Sargent
Mark Sheets
Mark Sztyber
Mark Tronco
Mark Troop
Mark Waters
Martha W Hood
Martin Brown
Martin Eric Rodgers
Martin Nathan

Mary Addonizio
Mary Clarke
Mary Heiss
Mary Tinebinal
Mary Wang
Maryse Meijer
Mathias Ruthner
Mathilde Pascal
Matt Davies
Matthew Cooke
Matthew Crossan
Matthew Eatough
Matthew Francis
Matthew Gill
Matthew Lowe
Matthew Woodman
Matthias Rosenberg
Max Longman
Maxwell Mankoff
Maya Feile Tomes
Meaghan Delahunt
Meg Lovelock
Megan Taylor
Megan Wittling
Mei-Ting Belle Huang
Mel Pryor
Melanie Stray
Michael Bichko
Michael Bittner
Michael Boog
Michael Eades
Michael James Eastwood
Michael Floyd

Michael Gavin
Michael Parsons
Michael Schneiderman
Michele Whitfeld
Michelle Mercaldo
Miguel Head
Mike Abram
Mike Schneider
Miles Smith-Morris
Mim Lucy
Miranda Gold
Molly Foster
Mona Arshi
Monica Tanouye
Morayma Jimenez
Moriah Haefner
Nancy Jacobson
Nancy Langfeldt
Nancy Oakes
Nancy Peters
Naomi Morauf
Nargis McCarthy
Nasiera Foflonker
Nathalie Teitler
Nathan McNamara
Nathan Weida
Niamh Thompson
Nichola Smalley
Nicholas Brown
Nicholas Jowett
Nicholas Rutherford
Nick Chapman

Sarah Brewer
Sarah Lucas
Sarah Manvel
Sarah Pybus
Sarah Stevns
Satyam Makoieva
Scott Chiddister
Sean Johnston
Sean Kottke
Selina Guinness
Severijn
  Hagemeijer
Shannon Knapp
Sharon Dilworth
Sharon
  McCammon
Sharon Rhodes
Sian Hannah
Sienna Kang
Silje Bergum
  Kinsten
Simak Ali
Simon Clark
Simon Pitney
Simon
  Robertson
Sophie Nappert
Stacy Rodgers
Stefano Mula
Stephan Eggum
Stephanie Miller
Stephanie
  Wasek
Stephen Fuller

Stephen Pearsall
Stephen Yates
Steve Clough
Steve Dearden
Steve Tuffnell
Steven Norton
Stewart Eastham
Stuart Grey
Stuart Wilkinson
Sujani Reddy
Susan Edsall
Susan Ferguson
Susan Jaken
Susan
  Wachowski
Susan Winter
Suzanne and
  Nick Davies
Suzanne
  Kirkham
Sylvie Zannier-
  Betts
Tania Hershman
Tara Roman
Tatjana Soli
Tatyana
  Reshetnik
Taylor Ffitch
Teresa Werner
Tess Lewis
Tess Lewis
The Mighty
  Douche
Softball Team

Theo Voortman
Thom Keep
Thomas Alt
Thomas Fritz
Thomas Noone
Thomas van den
  Bout
Tiffany Lehr
Tim Kelly
Timothy
  Cummins
Tina Rotherham-
  Winqvist
Tina Juul
  Møller
Toby Ryan
Tom Darby
Tom Doyle
Tom Franklin
Tom Gray
Tom McAllister
Tom Stafford
Tom Whatmore
Tracy Bauld
Tracy Lee-
  Newman
Trevor Latimer
Trevor Wald
Tricia Durdey
Turner Docherty
Valerie
  O'Riordan
Vanessa Baird
Vanessa Dodd

Vanessa
  Fernandez
  Greene
Vanessa Heggie
Vanessa Nolan
Vanessa Rush
Veronica
  Barnsley
Victor
  Meadowcroft
Victor Saouma
Victoria
  Goodbody
Victoria
  Huggins
Victoria
  Osborne
Vijay Pattisapu
Wendy
  Langridge
William
  Brockenborough
William Richard
William
  Schwaber
William Orton
William Wilson
Yoora Yi Tenen
Zachary
  Maricondia
Zoe Taylor
Zoe Thomas
Zoë Brasier